Triple-Dare to Be Scared

Thirteen Further Freaky Tales

Triple-Dare to Be Scared

Thirteen Further Freaky Tales

ROBERT D. SAN SOUCI

Illustrations by DAVID OUIMET

Cricket Books
Chicago

Library of Congress Cataloging-in-Publication Data

San Souci, Robert D.
  Triple-dare to be scared : thirteen further freaky tales /
Robert D. San Souci ; illustrations by David Ouimet. — 1st ed.
      v. cm.
  Contents: Second childhood — They bite, too! — Plat-eye — Tour
de force — Underwater — Far site — Field of nightmares — The
double — John Mouldy — Green thumb — *El arroyo de los fantasmas*
— Bookworm — Rain.
  ISBN-13: 978-0-8126-2749-7
  1. Horror tales, American. 2. Children's stories, American.
[1. Horror stories. 2. Short stories.] I. Ouimet, David, ill. II. Title.
  PZ7.S1947Tri 2007
  [Fic] — dc22
                                        2006025899

contents

second
Childhood

The baseball game Saturday afternoon was rained out—
flooded out, really—though the boys managed to play three
innings. But when water pooled around the bases and
turned the outfield into a lake, the players gave up, heading
for home. Most of the boys lived in the housing develop-
ment close to the park. Daniel Scott, who went to the same
school as the others, lived a mile down the road, in the
older part of Pine Grove on Leesmark Island, off the coast
of Georgia.

As the others reclaimed their bikes or raced away on
foot amid cries of "See ya!" Daniel mounted his own bike.
A flash of lightning, followed by a huge roll of thunder,
made him pump his feet harder. Lightning and thunder
terrified him. He was equally frightened and angry with

himself for not splitting when the storm had begun. Now he was out in the open, with lightning that seemed to be following him as he pedaled down the road.

The rain was getting worse. He was soaked; even his Adidas were getting squishy. And the wind was driving the rain into his face, blurring his glasses. He could barely see the road. Fortunately he saw the sign for Creekside Lane. He never traveled the road because it went past the cemetery by Old First Church—a place that had frightened him ever since he had been a toddler, and older kids had teased him with frightful stories about the place. But he knew some of his friends used it as a shortcut to Forest Lane. Daniel's home was at the end of the second lane. Steering with one hand, he pulled his glasses off and tried to wipe them on his sopping jacket. He peered through the rain, but his bad eyes and the rain-veils left him practically blind. He replaced the nearly useless glasses, relieved to spot no on-coming headlights.

Then, as he sped past Old First Church, he hit a water-filled pothole. The front wheel of his bike twisted sharply right, spilling him onto the gravel at the road's edge, knocking the wind out of him. For a few moments, he lay stunned, half covered by the bright red bike. His right shoulder and elbow, which had taken most of the fall, hurt badly. He could feel individual bits of gravel pressing into his cheek. Afraid that a car might come roaring down the road from behind and not spot him sprawled there, he climbed shakily to his feet and dragged his bike off the road, under the branches of a pine that protected him from the worst of the rain. He pressed his shoulder and elbow, feeling for injuries, then flexed his right arm. It hurt, but nothing seemed broken or sprained.

His bike was a mess: the front tire was bent and angled sharply away from the frame. Daniel tried forcing it back into alignment, but the damage was too much to fix without tools. He tried to push the bike, but there was something wrong with the chain; both wheels refused to turn.

Violet-tinted lightning zigzagged across the sky. Daniel suddenly remembered from Scouting that sheltering under a tree was not a good idea.

Then the rain slackened enough for him to see that he was only a short distance from one of the black iron gates in the chest-high stone wall guarding the churchyard beyond. He had always avoided the place, with its headstones tilting this way and that and the hulking shapes of the old-fashioned mausoleums — the small stone houses for the dead. Now some of the tombs, with their little roofed porches, promised better shelter than the tree branches overhead.

Another crackle of lightning — seeming much closer — decided for him. Abandoning his bike, he pushed through the rusting gate.

The two nearest mausoleums offered little protection from wind and rain; the third had a foot and a half of projecting porch roof. He took refuge there, leaning against the heavy iron door to get as much cover as he could.

To his surprise, the door swung inward, nearly landing him on his butt. Only his quick reaction in throwing

3

himself forward kept him from a bone-jarring jolt.

Breathing heavily from his near mishap, he stared into the shadowy space beyond. Some light filtered through barred openings near the stone ceiling. There weren't the expected coffins; the space was empty. His curiosity overcoming his uneasiness, he took a couple of steps inside. Now he could see a rectangular opening in the floor. Cautiously, he approached it, leaning forward for a better look, his whole body tensed and ready to run if anything stirred in the darkness.

Fumbling in his pocket, he pulled out the little flashlight on his key chain. He snapped it on; the high-intensity beam revealed a steep, narrow, water-stained flight of steps plunging down into deep darkness.

He listened but could hear nothing beyond the pelting rain, the rush of wind, and unnervingly loud peals of thunder. He thought, *Exploring this place — just a little — would be something to boast about to my friends. I might even triple-dare them to do the same.* Since he was sure they would never take the dare, this would boost his standing in the group. He'd take a quick look — just get some sense of what was down there. Then he could make up some gory details.

Slowly, alert for a telltale sound or movement, he followed the light beam down into the blackness. The stairs only descended about seven feet. Then he found himself in a second chamber about the same size as the one above.

He flashed his light around. Here were the expected coffins, stacked in niches on four sides.

He decided he'd seen enough. He started to turn back

when there was a rustle, a creak, a *whisper* that came from the newest-looking coffin directly across from the steps. The brass handles still gleamed; the reddish wood had a freshly waxed look. He suddenly remembered picking out a coffin two years before with his father just after his mother died. But this one was smaller. A child's coffin—one that would fit one of his friends—*or myself,* he thought uneasily.

There was another *creak.* A dark line appeared under the coffin lid. It looked as if it were being raised from inside, just like in the old vampire movies he watched when he stayed overnight at his friend Tyler's house.

The shadowy line widened. Somebody—*something*—was definitely pushing up the top half of the heavy rosewood lid.

Part of his brain was screaming, *Get out!* But his limbs were locked in terror. He remembered Tyler telling him the story of Old Man Dinkens, who refused to believe he had died, dug himself out of his grave, and sat on the cemetery wall, talking to passersby and falling to pieces until his wife insisted he be buried a second time.

Four thin white worms crept from under the lid, followed by a fifth, thicker one. *Maggots,* was Daniel's first thought. His stomach gave a lurch. Then, to his greater horror, he realized that he was looking at four bony fingers and a withered thumb. Something was definitely stirring in there, one hand seeking purchase on the side of the coffin, while the other continued to push up—weakly but determinedly—on the resisting lid.

The fingers were drawn back inside. The lid continued its slow rise.

Movemovemove his brain commanded his paralyzed legs. Something connected. He managed a step backward, then another, but he was unable to take his eyes off the terrifying sight in the niche before him.

Then the resistant lid was suddenly flung back as though by a desperate burst of strength. It hit the back of the niche with a *bang* and remained partly upright.

In the circle of his penlight, a shape slowly raised itself to a sitting position inside the half-opened coffin.

A delicate, pale face floated up—the skin stretched drum-tight, highlighting the cheekbones and forehead ridges. The eyes were black smudges. The mouth was smiling, but the hands reached up and struggled to loosen whatever inside the mouth was keeping the grin in place.

Something was pulled free. Daniel's hands were shaking so much that the light was bobbing all over, giving the corpse's movements a herky-jerky quality that was all the more frightening as the eyes, like thumbholes pushed into cookie dough, locked on his.

The mouth—a slit in skin so paper-thin, Daniel expected it to split at the corners—moved in an effort to shape words. A raspy voice whispered, "Want to play?" The horror began to climb free, using the lower half of the coffin lid to lever itself up and out.

"No!" Daniel bellowed, finding his own voice and snapping free of the fear lock on his legs and arms. He flung his flashlight at the thing, heard a soft *thunk*, like metal hitting plastic. Then the sturdy little light fell to the floor and rolled to a stop, its beam slanting across the lower steps leading to safety.

Not daring to look back, Daniel scrambled up the steep, slippery stairs. Above his panting and grunting, he heard the something drop to the crypt floor, then shuffle toward the stairs.

He redoubled his efforts, so eager to escape the darkness and what it held that he stumbled on the top step, sprawling full-length onto the stone floor near the still-open door. His nylon Windbreaker did nothing to cushion the pain in his arms and elbows. He felt the left knee of his jeans tear. Ignoring his scraped hands, he got to his feet and hurtled out into the downpour, risking a single glance behind him. A lightning flash revealed a black-and-white figure framed in the doorway.

He splashed through puddles, driven by fear of lightning — and of something *much worse.* His bike was forgotten; he was lurching through the blinding rain, trying to remember the way back to the cemetery gate. From time to time he swiveled his head around to see if the thing was following him, but the rain made it impossible to see.

Then, somewhere far ahead, he spotted another gate, swinging back and forth in the wind. Just beyond, he saw a rectangle of light — a house window! With a sob of relief, he hurried toward it, at every moment expecting a withered hand to fall on his shoulder.

He could see the house now, across a thin strip of road, guarded by a rotting wooden fence that pitched this way and that. Huge moss-covered oaks pressed in upon the place. It was three stories tall and looked unpromisingly gray and dilapidated. Since he had never been on this side of the cemetery, he had no idea who might live here.

He raced up the sagging steps and pounded on the door with both fists. "Help! Someone is after me." Continuing to bang with one fist, he turned to peer into the worsening rain. He could spot no sign of his pursuer but fancied he saw a dark, slow-moving shape among the rain-blurred grave markers.

"Please!" he shouted, redoubling his assault on the door.

"Who's there?" a timid voice asked from inside.

"Let me in!" Daniel pleaded, slumping against the door. "He—*it*—is going to get me." Now he was sure he saw a darker shadow moving toward him through the downpour.

"I'm not supposed to open the door when my parents are gone," the voice answered.

"I'm just a *kid!*" Daniel shouted. "You sound like you're about my age."

"My father is really strict." But the voice sounded less sure.

Daniel glanced away. Surely—*surely*—he saw something at the edge of the cemetery backlit by the most dazzling lightning flare yet.

"Please, please, please," he begged one last time.

The door opened abruptly. Instantly Daniel darted inside and slammed the door behind him.

"How do you lock it?" he demanded.

"Turn the latch this way." Out of the shadows of the hall, a boy's pale hand, smaller and slimmer than his, reached over and locked the door with a satisfying *click*.

"Thanks!" said Daniel, letting his eyes adjust to the semidarkness, where watery light filtered through matching frosted glass panels on each side of the door. But the lights were on in the living room, set off from the hall on the left by a half-closed pocket door.

Now his rescuer came into focus: a black-haired boy with eyes as dark as his hair. He looked about two years younger than Daniel. "You're not going to hurt me, are you?" he asked, taking a step backward.

"No way," Daniel assured him, stepping into the comforting light. "But there's something scary out there." He crossed to the nearest window, twitched the curtain aside just enough to survey the yard, the road, and the cemetery beyond. He could make out nothing for certain, but rain and wind and lightning made everything seem to move.

"Where's your phone? Um—what's your name?"

"Leonard," the boy muttered so softly that Daniel could barely understand.

"Kids call you Len or Lenny?"

"Leonard. My folks don't like nicknames."

"O.K., *Leonard*, where's the phone? The phone, the phone," he repeated impatiently, since the other boy seemed thrown by the question.

The boy pointed to an old-fashioned black cradle phone on a little table inside the lighted hall door.

Daniel grabbed it. The phone crackled with static. He wasn't sure he heard a dial tone. But he frantically dialed 911. The phone hissed loudly, but there was no ringing at the other end. He pushed the plungers, waited a moment after the line went dead, then released the plungers, letting the phone crackle back into static-y life. He dialed the emergency number again. No response. A blaze of lightning filled the windows with brightness. Simultaneously the phone gave a high-pitched screech, making him hold the receiver at arm's length. When the earsplitting sound died away, he raised it cautiously to his ear. Dead silence — not the ghost of a dial tone. He pressed down repeatedly on the plungers. *Nada.*

Great. Just great, he thought. *Lightning probably fried the wires.*

"You got a cell phone? A computer? Any way we can call for help?"

The other boy shook his head. "Just . . ." He waved his hand at the useless phone. Daniel slammed the receiver back onto its cradle.

There was an answering crash from the porch outside as something fell. Daniel hoped it had been blown over — not pushed.

"Are all the doors and windows locked?" Daniel asked.

Leonard nodded. "My folks are real strict."

"When will they be back?" asked Daniel, looking quickly past the curtain. Leaves and small branches scudded across the porch. Their scratching sounds made him think of withered fingers dragged along window glass, probing at door handles — *looking for a way in.*

He wondered how long it would be before his father realized he was missing and called the police. He imagined one of the sheriff's patrol cars drifting down the lonely lane past the house. The boys could flag it down, and they'd both be safe. Of course, half the time his father just came home, collapsed into his chair, flicked on the television, and fell asleep, exhausted from work. He might sleep till ten or eleven o'clock before waking and realizing that something was wrong. Daniel and his father had drifted apart in recent months. Now he wished the man were here to protect him from the nightmare he sensed lurking in the thickening twilight outside and made worse by the relentless rain.

"Want to play?" asked Leonard.

The words startled him; even spoken softly, they made him jump.

"Sorry I scared you."

Embarrassed, Daniel just asked, "Play what? What games have you got? Doom? Resident Evil?"

"Scrabble. Snakes and Ladders. Monopoly." After a minute he added hopefully, "Checkers?"

"No GameBoy or Xbox?"

Leonard shook his head and looked ready to cry.

What a wimp, thought Daniel, feeling irritated and at the same time sad because the other seemed so helplessly out of it. He might as well be angry at a puppy, he decided. "Checkers. Fine," he said aloud.

"They're in my room; we can play up there."

"Can you see the road out front from your bedroom?" He was thinking of watching for a police car — any car — that might come down the lane.

"Yes," said Leonard, leading the way.

They were halfway upstairs when all the windows burned

white-hot with the worst lightning flare yet. When the glare died away, so did the light on the stairs and in the living room. The stairway was suddenly as black as the stairs in the mausoleum.

"Leonard!" Daniel hissed, instinctively stretching his hand toward the shadow two steps above him. The other boy's fingers—cool, dry, thin—circled his own and gently tugged him upstairs.

"I have candles in my room," the younger boy said. "The power goes off a lot."

There was enough light sifting in through windows at either end of the upstairs hall that Daniel felt O.K. to pull back his hand before following Leonard into the corner bedroom. One generous window looked across the side yard to the cemetery beyond; Daniel shuddered but eyeballed every bit of the scene. He saw nothing beyond rain-shrouded tombs and gravestones and trees whipping in the wind.

Leonard's mom wasn't much of a housekeeper—dust and cobwebs overlay everything—but then neither was Daniel's father.

The other window gave a clear view of the lane in front of the house, from where it emerged out of the trees until it was swallowed by a second grove. No sign of headlights. Daniel settled down, leaning his shoulder against the wall. Leonard set out candles on the dresser and window sills.

"Good," Daniel approved, imagining the candle shining out like a beacon, pulling help closer. The candlelit room seemed *almost* safe and cozy. But he couldn't stop imagining hands that were hardly more than bone covered with dried, papery skin endlessly circling the house — touching, patting, probing, seeking a way in.

They played checkers, but Daniel kept losing: he was more concerned with watching for cars on the road. His ears were alert for any sound out of the ordinary. Besides, the game bored him as much as it delighted the other player. His legs were cramping from sitting on the floor. He was also getting hungry and thirsty.

"You got anything to eat?" he asked. "Any soda?"

"It would be in the kitchen," Leonard said uncertainly. "At the end of the hall downstairs."

"I'll find it," Daniel said, relieved to stand up and get away from jumping red and black plastic checkers around the board. "You want something?"

"No. I'll stay and set up the next game." Daniel was getting impatient with the other boy's fondness for the stupid game — and with his puppylike need to be reassured, asking endlessly, "Are you having fun? It's fun, isn't it? Just us two and the rain outside."

And something much worse, Daniel thought, but he didn't say anything. He'd warned Leonard; Leonard didn't seem to care. And the fact that nothing frightening had happened once he had found shelter was lulling him — a tiny bit — into a feeling of safety.

But his unease quickly returned as he made his way cautiously and silently downstairs. He froze every time a stair squeaked underfoot. When he was far enough down to see several windows, he looked out each one for a hint of shadow or flicker of movement. But he saw nothing.

Moving stealthily down the hall, he eased open the door at the end.

Unwashed dishes crusted with food and layered with dust in an old-fashioned porcelain sink were further proof of what a bad housekeeper Leonard's mother must be. There was grit on the floor; it made a scratching noise underfoot.

He opened the refrigerator, figuring the power hadn't been off long enough to warm any cold drink inside. The smell when he opened the door nearly gagged him: spoiled meat, soured milk and cottage cheese, and rotting vegetables turning to liquid in their plastic bins made it clear that no one had checked things out for weeks. There were no soft drinks—which made him angry with the other boy for getting his hopes up. *What a loser!* he decided.

He wondered how long Leonard's parents had been gone.

Had something happened to them? That would explain the dust and dirt and spoiled food. But Leonard didn't seem upset. Still, there was something odd, something almost simpleminded about the boy who wasn't concerned as to what had driven Daniel to take refuge in the house, who didn't seem to notice that his parents might have abandoned him, who only wanted to play checkers or other baby games.

Daniel opened the cupboards, still looking for something to eat, and found a tin of chocolate chip cookies that turned out to be not too stale. He found a glass, rinsed the dust off it, and drank some tap water. When he looked out the window above the sink, it seemed to him that the storm was dying down a bit. The lightning and thunder seemed to have moved inland and were flickering and rumbling less often. Now if only the police or his dad or even Leonard's parents would turn up . . .

He decided to take the rest of the cookies upstairs. He put his arm out to push open the kitchen door that had swung shut when he heard a faint sound from behind what he thought was a closet door. For a minute, his heart nearly stopped; then he heard the miserable mewing of a cold, hungry cat. Somehow the thing had gotten shut in the closet. Daniel decided to let it free and give it some food (somehow he couldn't imagine Leonard taking the time), figuring dry or tinned cat food would still be good to eat. "Easy, kitty," he called, turning the knob on the closed door.

But it wasn't the door to a closet; it was a laundry room. Against one wall were a washer and dryer. Against the other wall were twin old-fashioned gray concrete tubs. The cat he'd come to rescue—black with three white paws—meowed at him from the top of a cabinet stacked with powdered soap, bleach, and other laundry aids.

Daniel took this in at a glance, hardly letting it register; his eyes were drawn to the far end of the narrow room where a door stood open to the backyard. Wet, wind-driven leaves were swirling in and mixing with drifts of soap powder on the floor. Something—the cat?—had knocked a box

33114015883275

of detergent off the end of the dryer. Wind had scattered the powder across the linoleum. Wind . . . and something else. In the spilled soap were two faint lines—not really footprints, but gouges in the powder—as if someone with small feet had shuffled through it. But nearer the kitchen door, the footprints became more clearly defined—as if the intruder grew surer-footed with each step. By the time the marks reached the kitchen door, faint prints of damp powder clearly revealed they had been made by someone with shoes the size of a child's. The clues suggested that someone had gone out the kitchen door, closing it or letting it blow shut behind him.

Feeling it was useless, Daniel nevertheless shut and threw the deadbolt on the outer door. The cat watched him intently. Without warning it leaped down onto the washer, hit the floor running, and raced into the kitchen. The sudden movement startled him; he dropped the round cookie tin, which rolled unnoticed under one of the washtubs.

Moving slowly, every nerve alert, Daniel peered into the kitchen. Now he understood the powdery grit he'd felt underfoot when he'd entered the room: it was the soap granule residue of someone's—some*thing's*—passage from the laundry room. Part of him—most of him—wanted to flee into the rain, abandoning the house to the monstrous thing. But that would mean leaving Leonard in grave danger.

Beyond the swinging hall door, faint traces of powder revealed that whatever had come in the back door had gotten at least this far—was now, he guessed, hidden somewhere in the house. He inched his way down the hall.

He wondered what had happened to the cat, which had vanished as completely as the intruder.

Suddenly, from the living room, he heard the cat yowl and hiss. Daniel bolted for the stairs, taking them two at a time. Downstairs, the cat screeched again.

"It's here! The scary thing's in the house!" he yelled to Leonard, who was kneeling in the candle glow, studying the checkerboard he had readied for the next game. Daniel slammed the bedroom door shut, fumbling with the knob. "How does it lock?" he asked.

"It doesn't. Only the bathroom has a lock. But that's broken." Leonard smiled up at Daniel. "Red or black?"

"Forget checkers!" cried Daniel. "Where's someplace safe with a door that locks?"

"The attic," said Leonard, smiling. He seemed glad to have the answer, happy to please his new playmate.

Daniel grabbed the boy's arm. "Show me."

There was a pitiful wail from the cat below — then sudden silence.

"What was that?"

"Your cat, but I think something just happened to it."

"I don't have a cat; I have a kitten. A black one with three white paws."

Daniel wasn't about to point out that the cat and the kitten had the same markings. "The attic," he hissed.

Leonard picked up the checker game. "That will be fun; I love to play up there."

Daniel bit back a shout — *This isn't a game!* — deciding the other kid was mentally out in la-la land — and therefore in

17

even more danger. He felt as if he were in charge of a kindergartner. All he said was, "Come *now!*"

They each took a candle. Daniel blew out the others and brought them, too. He didn't want to be without light anywhere in this house anytime during the night if he could help it.

Keeping watch on the head of the stairs, he followed Leonard to a narrow door near the hall's end. Daniel yanked the old-fashioned key, with a pattern of square teeth, out of the lock and half shoved Leonard into the dark stairwell beyond. The attic steps rose steeply, then turned sharply right halfway up. He handed his own candle to Leonard, three steps up, then pulled the door shut and inserted the key. The lock gave a satisfying *click*. Daniel put his ear to the door but heard nothing. In his overworked imagination, though, he saw a shadowy figure, specks of soap clinging to its shoes, climbing to the second floor, step by relentless step. Clutching the key, he headed for the top floor.

The gloomy attic ran the length of the house. There were grimy windows at each end of the tent-shaped space littered with furniture, boxes, trunks, suitcases, and other things, their usefulness outlived.

"I play up here sometimes," Leonard said. He pointed out a cleared area where an old throw rug lay in front of a low dresser with a sheet draped over the back. The space was littered with boxes of jigsaw puzzles and more wussy games. The ends of old candles were stuck in two old candleholders on the dresser. Daniel quickly replaced these with their lit candles.

Then Leonard thought of something. "Give me the key."

"Why?"

"It's my house," the boy answered stubbornly.

"Fine, take it," Daniel said, tossing it to the younger boy. "But swear you won't open the door unless I say it's O.K."

"Sure," said Leonard, pocketing the key.

Leonard sat on the rug and began unboxing the checkers. Daniel sat opposite him, not the least interested in playing. He was trying to come up with a plan. They were safe for the moment, but they had no food (he thought of the cookies left downstairs) or water. Leonard's parents were a mystery who could not be counted on. It would be up to his father and the police to find them somehow.

Daniel suddenly felt exhausted; he slumped back against the bureau. His eyes were drawn to the expanse of sheet looming above Leonard. "What's under that?"

"A mirror," said the other offhandedly.

"Great!" said Daniel, standing up. "It'll reflect the candles. We'll get more light."

"No!" said the other boy, grabbing at Daniel's arm. But he was too late: Daniel had already taken a fistful of the material and yanked. The dusty sheet slid to the floor. Daniel saw his image in the huge wood-framed oval mirror; the silver backing was scratched and foxed, but it still brightened the place.

He studied himself in the mirror, but he could only see the top of Leonard's head, the black hair so dark it seemed inky. He looked down at the boy hunched over the checkerboard, then back at the bit of his reflection.

They didn't quite match.

"Stand up," he said, his voice not much more than a whisper.

"No. You sit. Red or black?"

"Stand up!" Daniel insisted, putting real force behind his words this time.

"You won't be happy," said Leonard. But he stood up beside Daniel.

Daniel looked from Leonard to their reflections. The second figure inside the frame was the boy-thing from the crypt.

"You got here before me," said Daniel.

"I lived here before I died. But I didn't want to be dead. I just lay there in the dark. Then I felt you coming. I wanted a friend and I decided to come back and be a live kid again."

"The dead make their own rules," Daniel mumbled, remembering something he'd heard on TV.

"I didn't want to scare you, so I changed as much as I could. But I saw in the dining room downstairs that I couldn't fool a mirror."

Daniel said nothing.

"I have the key. You can't leave."

"My father. The police. They'll come." After a minute he added, "What about your mom and dad?"

"I think my folks went away because they were sad when I died. Maybe they've gone away forever."

"I'll break the door down. I'll get away." Daniel was talking to the grinning reflection.

"I don't think so." The reflected mouth moved, but the

words were spoken into his ear. "I'm stronger now than I was before." The fingers that had seemed so thin and stick-like earlier encircled Daniel's wrist like a handcuff. "You don't have any choice except 'red or black.' Now sit."

Daniel sat.

they bite,
too!

"I'd love to take a chunk of this island home with me. Then I could relive these two weeks the other fifty weeks of the year," Cole Trent's mother said.

"Never take anything away from this island except memories and souvenirs—they're all made in China anyhow," said their waiter in the hotel restaurant. He was a handsome *hapa*, mixed race, Hawaiian and Japanese.

The seriousness with which the fellow had responded to her joking comment threw Irene Trent. "Just kidding," she said, taking a quick swallow of after-dinner coffee to hide her flusterment. Cole's father, his mind no doubt wrapped up in details of packing and getting to the airport to catch the inter-island flight to Honolulu, the final flight back to California, didn't notice the exchange. He just smiled vaguely at his wife and sipped his coffee.

Cole, however, asked, "Why not? Couldn't I take just a rock or some shells or a pocketful of sand? Why would it hurt?"

"Take away enough, and there'll be no island left," said his father, in what Cole referred to as his "Professor Trent" voice, the voice he used at the college when he gave the lectures that Cole's mother sometimes dragged the boy to.

"And you'll make the *eepas* mad," said the waiter, refilling the adults' coffee cups.

"Eepas—what are they?" asked Cole. "I mean, I've heard of Menehunes, the little guys—sort of like elves or hobbits—on the Big Island."

"Menehunes are mostly harmless," said Dr. Trent, "though they can make mischief, according to some old stories. Actually, there may have been a race of small people who first settled the islands, and—"

Cole rolled his eyes at his mother, recognizing from the "Professor Trent" voice that his father was warming up to a lecture on Hawaiian history.

"Yes, darling," said his wife, placing a hand on his wrist and suggesting, "but you'd better finish your coffee so we can get back to the room and finish packing."

"Right-o," her husband agreed, his train of thought having been successfully switched to return-trip preparation.

But the waiter wasn't about to drop things. "What we got on Ilianu ain't Menehunes. Sometimes folks on other islands see Menehunes—even talk to them, I hear. No one never seen an eepa. Leastwise, no one who lived to tell.

They Bite, Too!

Closest you come is maybe you see something thin, brown, and *wiki wiki*—fast, *real fast*—outta the corner of your eye. Otherwise no one sees much of you again, 'cept maybe some chewed-up bones. Eepas got human hands and lizard feet. Their teeth is real bad. They bite. Bite you and never let go."

"How do you know if no one's seen them?" Cole asked skeptically.

"Folks know," the man answered.

"Sounds like stories of the Carkers," said the Professor, "man-lizard things that supposedly live in the California and New Mexico desert. They guard Indian and Spanish ruins and prey on lone travelers. Rumors describe them as small, quick, and lizardlike, with sharp teeth."

"Any more stories like these and none of us will sleep before getting on the plane," said Cole's mother, who dismissed the waiter with a terse, "We need our check."

But the waiter had one parting shot. He presented their bill saying, "The eepas are why you don't wanna take nothing home. They guard this island—every stone, tree, seashell. Anyone takes something, they follow. They get it back."

They bite, too, thought Cole. *These are just ghost stories to scare the* haoles, *non-natives,* he decided. But he had a sudden flash of guilt about the little statue he had hidden in his room.

While his parents packed, Cole retrieved the small idol rolled into one of his remaining pairs of clean socks. The figure was only about three inches high, carved from reddish black stone. It was old: a lot of the details had been worn away. It was hard to tell if it was supposed to be crouching or sitting on some kind of stool. It wasn't human. The hands, fisted and resting on the knees, hinted at claws, as did the bare toes. The humorless grin revealed serrated teeth like a shark's. The ears were only holes, and the nose was more like a snout. As he studied it, Cole was struck by how much the thing matched the waiter's description of an eepa.

The boy had found it while exploring a small cave hidden by a mass of lantana far down the shore from the hotel during one of his solitary treks. It had been sitting on a rock shelf. There were the dried remains of berries around it—almost like offerings. But it was clear from the undisturbed dust everywhere that no one had visited the cave for a long time.

He didn't show it to his parents. They would insist he leave it on the island. So it was his secret. When he heard his mother call him, he quickly hid his treasure.

He had a hard time sleeping. The excitement of the trip home, the rubbing and creaking of the tall koa trees outside his window, and remembered stories of the eepas kept sleep at bay. The koa tree sounds grew louder as the night wind rose. Over the soft hum of the air conditioner, he thought he heard the chatter of small voices, the scrabble of claws on branches. *Maybe I'll leave the statue behind tomorrow,* he thought. *Or maybe not,* he murmured to himself, imagining showing it off to his friends back home. In any case, the faint chattering and scrabbling subsided. The wind calmed. Cole slept.

In the morning sunlight, the spooky stories and his

imaginings of the night before seemed foolish. He carefully stowed the statue deep in his suitcase.

He watched the Grand Ilianu Hotel, with its awnings and polished balconies and gardens filled with eye-dazzling blossoms, vanish through the back window of the shuttle. Soon enough, the island itself disappeared behind the little island-hopper plane that took them to Honolulu. By late afternoon, they were in a 747, taxiing down the runway on the last leg of their journey home.

Cole's mother always got nervous during takeoff and landing, but once they were airborne, she was fine. Cole's father lived for the moment when he could pull out his laptop and work on a class lecture or a journal article.

For Cole, flying was never 100 percent comfortable. He had watched too many airplane disaster movies on cable. He had also watched *Twilight Zone: The Movie* way too many times. The "Nightmare at 20,000 Feet" segment—where a guy sees a gremlin, white and furry, like a mini–Abominable Snowman on the wing of the plane, ripping out the wiring to crash the plane—had connected deeply with Cole. From his seat, he couldn't see the plane's wings, but he was hyper-attuned to every click, creak, and groan the plane gave off. Always alert for a *different* sound. Yet he managed to sleep while his mother read and his father tapped the keyboard.

But sleep brought him his personal "Nightmare at 20,000 Feet." In the dream, he was looking out at the wing, where something crouched, ripping out the wing's guts. The creature was little and lean and deep brown; when it grinned at Cole, its lips curled back tightly from long and very scary teeth. The eyes were like polished black marbles, reflecting Cole's frightened features framed in the cabin window, his mouth moving soundlessly, unable to alert anyone to the danger.

Suddenly the thing abandoned its work, leaving a tangled mass of orange, red, blue, and green wires exposed like a frozen explosion midwing. Ignoring the streaming wind, it bounded in a human-lizard way to the double-paned window. The dead-black eyes locked on Cole's; the claws scraped at the plastic, easily peeling the superstrong material down in strips; the teeth chewed hungrily at the weakening outer panel of the double-paned porthole. In a moment, it had bitten through the outer window and was attacking the inner one, making short work of the second layer of tough polycarbonate. Its teeth shredded the plastic as fast as the claws scored it. In a moment, a tip of claw, a bit of tooth was through the second barrier.

Cole jerked back from the window, trying to shout but feeling his mouth and throat gum up, as though flooded with syrup. His dream self tried to rouse his mother, but she went on reading her book. Across the aisle, his father happily tapped away at the keyboard of his laptop. The flight attendant moved up and down, murmuring softly, handing out pillows and blankets. The aircraft dozed, unmindful of the horror chewing its way into the cabin.

I must scream now, I must scream now, dream Cole commanded himself.

He did scream his way into the waking world, into his

mother's comforting arms and his father's concerned but useless stare. The window beside him was unmarked.

"Bad dream?" Irene asked gently.

He nodded and shuddered.

"We'll be landing in San Francisco in an hour or so," his mother said. "Try to get a little more sleep."

But there was no way he was going to risk tapping into that dream again. It had been too real. He picked up one of the sports magazines he had bought at the airport, but he couldn't focus; his hands were so sweaty, they puckered the pages. He was even more aware than usual of sounds: shiftings in the overhead bins, scrabblings under his seat. Once he nearly jumped, feeling something brush his ankle, before deciding it was the guy behind him stretching his legs.

His suitcase was one of the last ones to come up onto the luggage carousel at the Oakland Airport. Cole found himself almost wishing it had been lost. Some lingering bit of nightmare clung to him. He kept imagining he saw thin, brown shapes out of the corners of his eyes. He assured himself that he was suffering from fatigue. But he had a growing sense of anxiety that centered on the statue hidden in his suitcase.

By the time they'd retrieved their car from long-term parking and driven to their home in the Oakland Hills, Cole was more and more regretting his decision to bring a little bit of Ilianu back with him. Their house, on a dead-end street surrounded by thick trees, seemed to him disturbingly isolated.

He unpacked quickly, shoving the sock with its worrisome burden deep into a drawer of his dresser. But as soon as he closed it, he thought he heard sounds from inside — faint chattering. He reached down to pull open the drawer, but he couldn't bring himself to touch the knobs. Instead he pushed a box of old books headed for the school rummage sale up against the drawer. Then he jumped into bed and pulled the covers up to his chin. The faint sound continued, just at the edge of his hearing, like the muttering he thought he had heard from the koa trees on their last night on Ilianu. It followed him into sleep, filling his dreams with images of swift, narrow shapes that moved too quickly to be seen clearly.

He felt as tired the next morning as he had when he went to bed. "Looks like someone is a little jet-lagged," his mother said as she served him bacon and eggs.

Still in his pajamas, he picked at his breakfast, not really hungry. "Where's Dad?" he asked.

"He went to the kennel to get Daisy Dawg; they should be back any minute."

Sure enough, a few minutes later the Australian shepherd bounded into the kitchen, with Cole's father following. She barked a greeting to Irene Trent, then zeroed in on Cole, still seated at the table, jumping up to lick his face, nuzzling under his hand to get petted. Cole slipped her a piece of his untouched bacon; she slugged it down in a single gulp.

"That's bad for her," said his father.

"I forgot to bring her a present from Hawaii."

"All right. But no more. Why don't you take her for a run? You look like it wouldn't hurt you to get your blood flowing, too."

"O.K.," Cole agreed. "C'mon, girl." Daisy Dawg followed happily, until he reached the bottom of the stairs. Normally it would be a race to the top, but now the dog stood with one paw on the bottom step. She cocked her head to one side and peered at the hallway above as if puzzled.

Cole, halfway up, yelled, "Come *on!*"

The dog followed uncertainly. On the threshold of Cole's bedroom, she froze. Her eyes locked on the bottom dresser drawer. Her ears flattened against the sides of her head. She bared her teeth and growled, deep and threatening—a sound that Cole had rarely heard from the good-natured dog.

He approached the drawer. Daisy Dawg's growl became a whine, but she reluctantly followed. With the dog behind him, Cole felt brave enough to open the drawer. He nudged the book box aside with his toe, reached down, and yanked the drawer open, ready to bolt if anything moved. A jumble of socks was all he saw. But at that moment, Daisy Dawg let out a horrible howl and streaked out of the room and down the stairs. Cole heard his parents' startled cries, then the slam of the back door as the animal escaped into the backyard.

A moment later, Cole's mother called up to him, "What happened to Daisy?"

"I don't know; she just *weirded out*," he shouted back. "It was like she smelled something in my room and it scared her. But there's nothing here. *Really.*"

"Do you think a raccoon got into your room while we were gone? Or into the attic space above your room? Ever since she got so badly mauled by that raccoon last year, I know the smell of one makes her crazy."

"There's no way a coon could've gotten into my room," the boy insisted.

"I'll have your father check the attic later," Irene said. "Go find Daisy, calm her down, and take her for that walk."

"Sure," said Cole. He knelt down by the open drawer, lifted out the special pair of socks, and unrolled the statue into his palm. It lay there, grinning up at him. The carving looked small and harmless, but he felt it was somehow connected to his troubling dreams, the dog's strangeness, and the sounds he could almost hear in the dark. What pleasure he had taken in smuggling the thing home was now replaced by fear.

He shoved the ugly thing back into the drawer, dressed, and went out to find his pet.

Outside, Daisy Dawg seemed fine, rolling playfully on her back in the grass that had grown tall while the family was away. They had a good ramble; Cole forgot his uneasiness. But Daisy Dawg hadn't forgotten her earlier distress. The closer they got to home, the more the animal tugged on the leash, pulled this way and that, seeming to do everything to keep them from returning.

It was a real tug of war to get her inside. She utterly refused to go upstairs, preferring to stay in the farthest corner of the family room.

Cole pushed open the door of his room. Something flickered at the corner of his vision. He had the impression of a small animal ducking under the bed. But the movement had been so quick, he couldn't be sure he'd seen anything. Moving cautiously, he picked up his baseball bat and, kneeling down, used the end of the bat to lift the edge of the bed skirt, prepared to scuttle backward if anything popped out. Nothing did. He circled the bed, raising the skirt on the other side. Nothing.

The sudden scuttering of tiny claws across the roof overhead jolted him. Then he recognized the sound of squirrels—something he heard several times a day. He dropped down on his bed, folding his legs under him rather than letting them dangle too close to the shadowy space under the bed. He still felt vaguely uneasy about what he thought he had seen earlier.

The squirrels returned. But something was wrong. The scampering sounds were coming from his closet—not the roof. *Our house is turning into a zoo,* he thought. But there was no way squirrels could have gotten into his room any more than raccoons. Hefting the baseball bat again, he opened the closet and tugged the chain to turn on the bulb. Again nothing. But something wasn't right. A puff of air tickled his hair. He stretched his hand up and felt a breeze. Getting a flashlight and stepladder from the hall closet, he checked further. A hole had been gnawed through the dry wall, just below the closet ceiling. Looking through the squirrel-sized opening, he saw a bit of roof. Clearly the creatures had chewed in from under the overhang of the second-story roof. His father wasn't going to be happy about the damage.

Cole pulled out a couple of small storage boxes to check for damage. He recoiled when his fingers touched something small and hard and wet and furry. Yanking his hand back, he knocked several containers off the shelf. The flashlight beam revealed a pile of bones mixed in with matted fur. The boy instantly recognized the remains of two squirrels. In horrified fascination, he peered closer. The bones looked gnawed. Whatever had killed the squirrels had eaten them. Did raccoons eat things like squirrels? He knew they had emptied their neighbor's pond of koi. Could a raccoon fit through the opening? Maybe the squirrels had died of injuries or sickness and crawled in here to die and then had been eaten by mice or roof rats, which were rumored to have taken up residence in the area.

Since it was Sunday, the exterminators couldn't be called to check things out. His father put the remains in a large plastic bag and set them in the toolshed in the far corner of the backyard. Daisy Dawg growled when Cole's father crossed the family room with the plastic bag, then backed as far away as she could. His father nailed a board across the opening as a temporary repair.

But though his mother scrubbed and disinfected the shelf, a faint, unpleasant odor seemed to linger in Cole's imagination, if not in fact. He kept the closet door firmly shut the rest of the day.

His sleep was tormented with nightmares of sharp-toothed, slim-shanked shapes gnawing into the windowless and doorless room in which his dream-self was trapped. Shark eyes peered at him from above lizard grins; all the while razor-sharp teeth and deadly claws ripped through the plasterboard walls faster and faster. This time he was too helpless to will himself awake. He could only watch as thin forms slithered free of the wall, dropped by dozens to the floor, and began circling him, jaws snapping with gruesome click-clacks.

The first one sank its fangs into his ankle. Pain—too real to be imagined—made him scream his way back into the waking world. It took him a minute to orient himself and a few more minutes to find the courage to uncurl from a protective ball buried deep under the covers.

When he emerged, he checked his ankle. He was startled to find that there was a red welt, like a spider bite, in the exact spot he'd dreamed. But there were no teeth marks— just redness. Whatever had bitten him may have done it the day before, and the irritation had later made him dream about being bitten. He decided to believe this rather than think about other possibilities.

He went downstairs, where he found his mother at the front door calling and whistling for Daisy Dawg.

"I haven't seen her all morning." Irene sounded worried. "Her food dish is untouched; looks like she went out the pet door and never came back." Turning, she said, "Eat some breakfast, then help your father look for Daisy. He took the car to go around the block, but he should be back soon."

"You O.K.?" Cole asked.

"I didn't sleep well," she explained. "Sounds in the walls, on the roof. Squirrels or mice, I suppose. Guess they decided to make themselves at home while we were away."

Cole ate some cereal and toast. Since his father hadn't returned, he decided to look for the dog on his own. He knew she loved to push through a loose board in the back fence and explore the little patch of trees that made a common area between their fence and the fences of households on the street behind. Once in a while the neighbors got together to thin the brush and do a general cleanup. But most of the time, the patch of green was left to grow wild.

Cole shouldered aside the board and squeezed through the tight opening into tall grass and bushes. He called the dog's name over and over, but though he heard lots of rustling and scuttling in the brush and around the roots of the pine and sumac and oleander that cluttered the area, no Daisy Dawg came bounding to him.

He had just made up his mind to leave when he spotted a patch of black-gray-white under a bush. He didn't have to get much closer to be sure it was the remains of his pet. He ran shouting for his parents.

"Raccoons," said the animal-control officer. "They chewed that poor pup all to—oh, sorry!" he said, realizing that Irene Trent was frantically signaling him to spare the gory details. "I can set some traps. Humane. Catch-and-release. If they've gotten this vicious, you don't want them around kids. Could be rabid," he added, lowering his voice.

"I'll talk to the neighbors; we can split the costs. Just send the bill to me," Cole's father said. His voice was shaking. The loss of the dog seemed to affect him more than Cole would have expected. Maybe he hadn't slept well, either.

The animal-control officer took the remains away "for a closer look." He promised to dispose of them respectfully. Cole felt vaguely that they should have done something more for Daisy Dawg, but he was relieved to have the carcass removed. He felt guilty; in his mind, the dog's fate was somehow linked to the unlucky statue he had taken from Ilianu. *Could eepas have followed it all the way to California?*

He thought about telling his parents. But he doubted they'd believe him. And it would mean admitting he had taken the statue in the first place. His father, especially, would be angry about that.

One thing was clear: he'd have to get rid of the statue. But if he just threw it away, that might make the creatures *really* mad. What—or *who*—might be the next victim after Daisy Dawg? Him? His parents? These thoughts chilled him.

Somehow I've got to get the statue back to Ilianu, he decided. The answer was simple enough: mail it back.

He took the statue from his drawer, wrapped it carefully in bubble wrap, and packed it in a small, sturdy box.

While his parents were busy in other parts of the house, he slipped into the den. Receipts from their vacation were still in a tidy pile on his father's desk, including a business card from the hotel manager, Dennis Kahane, listing the Grand Ilianu's address.

Using a piece of his father's university stationery, he wrote:

They Bite, Too!

Dear Mr. Kahane,

This statue was taken by accident. It belongs on your island. Please put it back. There is a small cave on the shore about a half-mile north of the hotel. It's behind a big bunch of lantanas, near the bottom of the cliff, where those big red boulders have fallen together.

Sincerely yours,

(On impulse, he signed the letter,)

Michael C. Trent, Ph.D.

Then he took one of his father's mailing labels and addressed it to the hotel manager. Cole doubted Mr. Kahane would search out the cave — but just getting the thing back to the island should make everything right, he decided.

At the post office, he discovered he had just enough to send the package priority — nowhere near enough for express. Just handing the package over to the postal clerk gave him a great sense of relief. He pedaled home feeling better than he had since leaving Ilianu.

That night he slept deeply, dreamlessly.

A week later, everything was just a bad memory — except for the pain of losing Daisy Dawg, which the whole family felt.

Cole returned home late one afternoon. "It's me!" he shouted, not meaning to slam the door as loudly as he did. "Sorry!" he called, anticipating his mother's "How many times have I asked you not to do that?" from the den where she worked at her Web site design business.

There was only silence. "Mom?" he called.

Nothing.

He started down the hall, then halted. The framed Japanese prints lining the wall were tilted every which way. One had fallen to the floor, smashing the glass. Suddenly frightened for his mother, he called again, louder, "Mom!"

No answer.

Half afraid to look, he peered through the open door of the den. The place was a wreck. The chair in front of the darkened computer screen had fallen over on its back, as though his mother had stood up suddenly. Books and papers were strewn all around. Pieces of a vase lay shattered amid lilies scattered against the baseboard. There was a wet splash mark about a foot and a half above the floor—as if someone had thrown the vase at something not very tall.

Amid the debris nearest the computer work station was a frighteningly familiar shape. Cole instantly recognized the box he had mailed off a week before. He picked it up in his shaking hands. It had been crunched; one corner was ripped open, the hole sloppily mended with packing tape. Most of the label had been torn off—except for the return address. Two purple-ink messages had been stamped on it: "Damaged in handling" and "Return to sender." He shook the box. It rattled—but it didn't sound right. Grabbing the scissors—still by the computer where his mother kept them—he cut open the box. Inside was a wad of bubble wrap, a piece of crumpled newspaper, and a plastic windup toy like a kid would get with a McDonald's Happy Meal.

The statue had been lost or stolen. Someone had just shoveled whatever was around into the damaged box and resealed it. In despair Cole realized that, in all likelihood, the statue would never be found. And if it was not returned to Ilianu, what would happen to him, to all of them? Leaving the box on the desk, he started in search of his mother—then froze.

Something stirred behind the computer unit. He heard a crackle of electricity. The computer screen flared into multicolored static, the power surged, and the electricity blew, taking down the computer and overhead light, plunging the room into semidarkness, since his mother kept the shades drawn when she worked at the computer.

Something rippled behind the floor-length curtains. It chattered and was answered by something under the sofa opposite the computer.

"Mom!" he bellowed, making a break for the door. His cry was as much a call for help as a warning.

Something fell heavily in one of the upstairs bedrooms. He paused at the bottom of the steps, uncertain what to do. Then he was sure he heard his mother's voice—very faint—calling his name. He hurried up, taking the stairs two at a time. In the upstairs hall, he called again. An answering cry sounded from his parents' bedroom.

In the bedroom was more of the disarray he'd seen downstairs. Things had been knocked off the dresser; his mother's jewel case had burst open, scattering its contents—as though the heavy lacquer chest had been slammed down at something. The bedside landline phone had been pulled apart, its wires bitten through. The quilt on the bed had been slashed as though a pack of animals had savaged it. The door to the bathroom was closed, but the wood at the bottom had been scratched and chewed as though some creature had tried to force its way through.

He tried the handle. Locked. He tapped lightly on the door. "Mom," he said softly.

"Cole?" After a moment, the lock clicked, then the door opened a crack. His mother pulled him quickly inside and locked the door behind them.

She looked awful. Her hands and feet—she was wearing sandals—were cut and bleeding. She could barely stand on one foot; her ankle was red and swollen.

"Are you O.K.?" he asked, though he could clearly see she wasn't.

"They bite," she said, "and they hang on—like snakes or lizards that keep their teeth clamped on a person even after they're dead." Irene shuddered. "What are they?"

"Eepas," he replied.

"Those Hawaiian things we heard about on Ilianu?" She shook her head. "Eepas are just a story." But he could see from the fear in her eyes that she knew he was telling the truth.

"Whatever you call them, they're there. I think they've been waiting for me." He explained everything.

"What are we going to do?" she asked, grabbing his wrist. It frightened him all the more to see her so terrified and helpless.

He looked at his watch. "Dad should be home in an hour."

"We've got to warn him or he'll walk into those things."

"They wrecked the phone in your bedroom. Where's your cell phone?"

"In the den. They surprised me. Suddenly they were all around me. I threw a vase. Then I tried to get to the front door, but they cut me off. So I ran up here." She paused. "It all started when that box came in the mail. I didn't open it. I didn't have a chance."

He shook his head. "It wouldn't have mattered. The post office lost the statue. Now I don't know what those things want. Maybe revenge."

"There must be something we can do." She went to the window and peered out at the roof, then groaned. When Cole looked, he saw six of the lizard shapes stretched out on the roof, their glittering black eyes fixed on the window with the intensity of hunting dogs that have treed their quarry.

"Maybe I can call for help." She hobbled over to the window and started to crank it open. The noise sent the creatures into a frenzy. They leaped up, jaws snapping, scrabbling for a hold on the window ledge. His mother hastily closed the window.

She sank down on the edge of the tub and put her head in her hands.

There was a thump, then a scratching at the window. Cole and his mother jumped. One of the things had reached the window ledge and was alternately raking its claws down the glass and digging at the aluminum frame, searching for a way in. It wouldn't take them long, Cole guessed. He opened the medicine chest, looking for a weapon—but the best he could find were nail scissors and a file. He handed them to his mother.

"These won't stop them," she said.

"They're better than nothing," he insisted.

He heard the sound of a car outside. Looking through the window, he was almost on eye level with the creature perched on the ledge. It turned to see what Cole was looking at. They both saw his father's Toyota starting up the drive. The creature barked something and was answered by a chattering below. Cole heard a clattering of claws on shingles. He had the stomach-churning sense that they were going to ambush his father.

He made up his mind on the spot.

Taking a deep breath, he yanked open the bathroom door.

"Cole!" his mother screeched. She made a grab for him, but her ankle buckled under her. With a cry, Irene fell back, grabbing the basin for support. Cole slammed the bathroom door behind him. Fearfully he looked around the bedroom, but saw no sign of the eepas. The hall was empty. He moved quietly to the head of the stairs, hearing his father shut off the engine of the Toyota. A moment later the driver's door slammed.

Cole was halfway down the stairs when he saw more than a dozen of them standing on their hind legs, too-human hands clasped in front of them, as if they were at prayer. Their shiny black eyes fixed on him; their mouths curved into frightful, toothy grins.

"Look, I'm sorry I took the statue. I wish I could give it back, but I can't. You . . . took our dog. Won't that be enough?"

They remained grinning up at him.

Slowly their grins widened.

Waiting.

"I don't have it anymore," he said helplessly, his mouth and throat as dry as paper.

Their grins nearly split their heads in two, revealing row upon row of bared teeth.

Still they remained frozen in place, like a row of tiny idols. Early evening sun filtering in the front windows shone bright on their thinness; their teeth contrasted whitely with their brown faces.

Then four things happened: Cole's mother lurched to the top of the stairs, clinging to the banister for support, crying his name; Cole took a step backward, up to the next higher step; his father's key turned in the front door lock. . . .

The eepas moved — *wiki wiki* — too fast for Cole to follow, only, an instant later, to feel.

plat-eye

On Saturday, the twins, Kazija and Kwame, were left in the care of their grandmother Burkett, their mother's mother. The ten-year-olds (Kwame was egged on by his older-by-eleven-minutes sister) had whined their way out of accompanying their parents, university professors who were collecting folk tales from the South Carolina Sea Islands and other areas, on another "field trip." This meant visiting old people scattered all across the coastal Low Country to hear stories about them and their ancestors. The children—mainly Kazija—had grown tired of spending long afternoons in hot, stuffy cabins and cottages while their parents questioned, listened, and recorded everything from family recipes to hand-me-down tales of slave times. This didn't interest the twins one bit.

The family had been staying on Mullaters' Island, where Louise's widowed mother, a retired schoolteacher, still lived in the house she had been born in. Her daughter and son-in-law had made the place their base of operations for the tale-gathering they hoped would be the start of a new book.

"Some 'vacation'," Kazija had complained to her twin the day before. "Nothing to do except be bossed around by Granny-Bee or listen to stupid, boring stories told by stupid, boring people."

"Sometimes they tell neat stuff," said Kwame. "You know — things about ghosts and witches and stuff. I liked that story about Jacky-My-Lantern whose wicked soul floats around like a candle forever, because the devil wouldn't let him into hell when he died. And those ghost lights in Morgan's swamp."

"I'd rather see a scary movie," said Kazija, waving her hand as if she could brush away the whole business. Having made up her mind, Kazija set to work getting what she wanted. She had taken whining to an art form. She also excelled at pouting and, when necessary, throwing tantrums. Kwame's efforts in these areas were just a faint echo of his sister's matchless skills at making their parents crazy and getting her own way.

What worked with their parents failed with Granny-Bee. The old woman dismissed the whines, pouts, and outbursts by insisting, "You're too old for such carryin' on, and I don't have time for this nonsense."

The twins were especially careful when they heard their

grandmother—who had just witnessed one of Kazija's confrontations—tell their mother, "Might be a good idea for you to take a switch to a certain backside. Put an end to that sass."

But Louise had simply said, "That's not the way Howard and I deal with things."

"Pardon my Low Country thinking," said the older woman tartly. "I forget you do things differently in Connecticut."

But this Saturday even being under the watchful eye of Granny-Bee seemed better to Kazija than riding up and down the coast, listening to endless old stories. "You don't want to go, either," she told her brother.

"I guess not," said Kwame, unwilling to disagree when Kazija was in one of her bad moods.

Their parents, eager to begin their hunt for old, narrative treasures, did not protest too much. Promising to be back in time for supper, they drove off, leaving the twins to do what they wanted. The only trouble was, there wasn't much to do at Granny-Bee's. Her home was nearly a mile from Glorietta, the nearest town. A few of the taller buildings could be seen above the piney woods that stretched from the edge of town and completely encircled their grandmother's house.

The day was too hot and humid for them to think of walking into town. When they asked their grandmother to drive them, she said, "I've got more important things to do than waste gas to amuse you."

"But there's nothing to do," said Kwame—stopping quickly when he realized he was whining.

"Shoulda thought about that earlier, before your folks left." She considered a bit, then said, "There are some chores around the house you could do."

The twins retreated quickly to the shaded back porch. Kwame took his dual-screen Nintendo out of his pocket, and they played with this for a while. But it wasn't much fun for the boy, since his sister's quick thinking and skilled fingers won every match—even when Kwame chose a game he was particularly good at.

They were in the middle of a round of Conquest when Kazija, whose turn it was, suddenly shut off the Nintendo. Kwame, who, by a stroke of luck, was a little bit ahead asked, "Why'd you do that?"

"I'm bored. Let's go down to the creek. We haven't been there yet."

"Mom and Dad never let us go there without one of them along."

"Well, they're not here. If you don't want to come, that's fine."

"We gotta ask Gran," Kwame reminded her. "You know her rules. If we just go off, she'll be mad, and I don't want her ticked off at me."

Kazija made a face, but she agreed. They went into the living room where their grandmother was sitting on the couch darning socks. Expecting a refusal, Kazija put on what Kwame called her "smiley face" and "syrupy voice" to ask the woman's permission to go to the creek.

To their surprise, the old woman was agreeable to the idea. "When I was no bigger than you, I remember spendin' many a sultry day down by the water." She smiled as though reliving some sweet memory. Then her face grew serious. "Only you be sure to take the dirt road to get there. And you come back the same way."

"Couldn't we just cut through the woods?"

"No! There's no clear path. Just deer trails that wind in and out and back on themselves. Folks are gettin' lost in there all the time. There's somethin' funny about those woods. When your grandfather was alive, he'd wallop the daylights out of the kids if they so much as set foot there. He always swore there was haints back there."

"Ghosts?" asked Kwame, thrilled and chilled at the same time.

"Worse," said the old woman. "Plat-eyes."

"What are those?" Kazija asked. "Some kind of animal?"

"Yes and no and mebbe," said the old woman, warming up to her taletelling. "See, a plat-eye is the ghost of someone who died and never got a proper buryin'. It's an *angry* ghost. And it can take any shape it wants. I heard tell of them lookin' like a dog or a cat or a horse. Might appear like a fella without a head. Sometimes it's just a dark cloud or hot smoke so thick it can suffocate a person."

"Why's it called 'plat-eye'?" Kwame asked.

"I've heard different reasons," Granny-Bee said. "The one that makes the most sense to me is that, when it gets close to you, it gets you in its power and its eyes get big and red and round as plates."

"Silly story," said Kazija. "Silly name."

Their grandmother just shrugged. "Stay out of those woods. That's all I'm sayin'."

"What happens if you do meet a plat-eye?" asked Kwame, ignoring his sister's eye rolling.

"Your only hope is to run away. But there is one bit of protection that can help."

She set aside her darning bulb and needle and got to her feet. "You two come with me," she said, heading into the kitchen.

Kwame looked at his sister. He saw from the way she raised her eyes and made a face behind Granny-Bee's back that she wasn't buying anything the old woman was saying. Kwame wished he didn't believe, yet his grandmother seemed so sure that he'd become convinced. But, not wanting to appear foolish in Kazija's eyes, he gave his sister a big, phony smile that said, *What a lot of baloney.*

In the kitchen the old woman began rummaging in a bottom drawer. Finding what she wanted, she pulled out two tiny bags sewn from scraps of burlap and held one out to each of the twins. They took them doubtfully. Kazija held hers up to her nose, then pulled it away quickly, holding it as far from herself as she could. "That stinks!" she said.

"It's just a little sulfur and gunpowder and a few other things," Granny-Bee explained. "This luck bag will help keep off any plat-eye. Just tuck it in your pocket."

"O.K., sure," said Kazija, shoving hers into her jeans. Kwame dropped his into his shirt pocket.

"Remember—follow the dirt road both ways. And don't set foot in those woods. And see you're back long before sunset. The moon is still young these days; a young moon sets spirits walkin'. Folks say plat-eye is at his worst on a night like that."

"We'll be careful," said Kazija, banging out the screen door in a rush. Her brother followed more slowly, careful not to let the screen door slam, since this annoyed his grandmother. They ran around to the front of the house and hurried down the tree-shaded driveway toward the country lane that would take them to the dirt road and, eventually, the creek. Kwame was sure his grandmother was watching them to see that they took the long way around.

As soon as they were out of sight of the old woman's cabin, Kazija pulled out her luck bag, pinched her nose, and announced, "Got to get rid of this stinky thing." She flung the packet into the bushes.

"I don't think you should have done that," said her brother.

"It's junk. It's giving you a stink—well, a *worse* stink. Don't hang around me if you've got that thing with you!"

Reluctantly, Kwame tossed his luck bag after his sister's.

Even taking the roundabout road, they reached the creek soon enough. While Kazija wandered up and down the bank, sometimes wading through a shallow spot, pausing to skip rocks across the water's surface or watch the flicker of a minnow or the progress of a crayfish across the pebbled creek bed, her brother contented himself by sitting in the generous shade of an ancient oak, playing his Nintendo.

"Don't you *ever* get tired of those stupid games?" asked Kazija a little later when she had given up her creekside explorations and sat on a flat stone, dangling her feet in the cool water. She used a palmetto leaf to brush away the flies and gnats that swarmed in the late afternoon. From time to time she probed the stony creek bed with a stick, hoping to stir up some crayfish or catfish action. To her disappointment, the water remained devoid of any activity.

"Uh-uh," her brother answered her question, without looking up. "It's sure more exciting than this place."

"How can that be?" the girl teased, mimicking Granny-Bee's voice. "Hereabouts, we got Jacky-My-Lanterns and ghost lights and plat-eyes and all sorts of haints." She left her seat by the water and approached her brother. He still didn't look up even when she poked him with the wet end of her stick.

"Cut it out!" He slapped the stick away, still not looking up from his game system.

Kazija suddenly hooked the end of her stick under the Nintendo, flipping it into the air. To the dismay of them both, it arced upward and landed with a *crack* of broken plastic on the sunbaked soil just beyond the oak's shade.

Kwame scrambled to his feet, shouting, "You *broke* it!" He ran to the Nintendo and picked it up. Frantically he tried to key life back into the shattered screen and darkened LED. But the thing was beyond repair. "Look what you did!" he bellowed, shoving the wreckage at his sister.

Kazija prudently backed away. She knew that she could usually bully her brother. But she also knew that when his temper engaged his fists, he was more than she could handle—was even sometimes more than their father could control. She had run afoul of the boy's windmilling arms and fists enough to know to move out of the danger zone as quickly as possible.

Kwame suddenly flung the broken Nintendo at her, barely missing her head. Then he was after her, arms frantically pounding the empty air.

His sister took off running along the creekbank, covering in haste the territory she had explored so leisurely earlier in the day. She easily navigated around brush and reeds. Behind her, she could hear Kwame yelling as he crashed through whatever stood in his way. From his shouts and the sounds of blind pursuit, she knew she was well advised to keep as far ahead of him as possible. Eventually, she knew, he would calm down; his anger would cool to mere spitefulness, and she would be able to reason him back under her influence. But not yet—no way yet!

Now she was charging into unknown territory, beyond the limits of her earlier explorations. Here the bank gradually sloped upward. Soon she was panting at the effort but still managed to keep up a good pace, staying safely ahead of her brother. She sensed his temper-fueled chase was easing as he fought his way through the thick undergrowth.

She put on a burst of speed, hoping to convince Kwame to abandon his efforts, when the ground suddenly gave way under her. She plunged down the almost vertical drop-off to an inlet through which a trickle of water fed into the creek. Screeching, she tried to slow her stumbling, but pitched downward, escorted by rocks and clods of earth.

She made a final, heroic effort to stop herself by thrusting her right foot forward. For a moment it seemed the ploy would work; then she slid on a small stone, felt her foot fold under her with a searing pain in her ankle, and she rolled the rest of the way to the bottom of the inlet. She came to rest in a muddy tangle of weeds beside the sluggish stream.

Dazed, Kazija sat up and gingerly touched her right ankle. Shooting pain erupted where she probed too deeply. She tried flexing her foot and ankle; the pain was awful, but she could move them. She hoped that meant nothing broken or torn, just strained and bruised.

"Kazija!" her brother shouted from overhead. He didn't sound angry anymore—just worried.

"Down here!" she called back. Still in a sitting position, she hitched herself free of the worst of the mud and weeds, not daring to try standing yet. A moment later, Kwame's face appeared over the brushy bank above.

"What happened?"

"You chased me so I fell," she said, figuring some guilt tripping would give her the upper hand. Just to make sure his temper was fully defused, and to maneuver him more completely under her thumb, she added, "My ankle could be broken. It's all your fault."

"You broke my Nintendo," he said stubbornly. But she could tell that the fire was out in him. Fear of what would happen if it turned out he had caused his sister serious injury took the last puff of wind out of his sails. "How can I help?" he asked. She heard concern and surrender in his voice.

"Get me out of here."

He found an easier, safer path a short distance back in

the inlet. Kazija just managed to stand by leaning heavily on his shoulder. At the foot of the trail, they found a thick, heavy branch that she used as a crutch. Her groans and yells during their ascent were only half-pretend.

Once they were on the high ground, her twin helped Kazija hobble back to the oak where the trouble had begun. They sat, backs to its trunk, considering what to do next.

"I could run back and get help," the boy suggested.

"Who? Granny-Bee? I don't think so. She'd call the sheriff or an ambulance and everything would get worse. And you know Mom and Dad aren't going to be back before dinner." She paused, noticing how the shadows of the trees on the far side of the creek had lengthened, stretching toward them across the water, marking just how late it was getting. "Besides," she said, "I don't want to stay here alone."

"You afraid?"

"Yeah," she admitted, then insisted hastily, "not of ghosts or stuff. But there are animals around."

"Then we're going to have to go together—if you think you can walk."

"Like I have a choice?"

He helped her to her feet.

"We'll cut through the woods," Kazija decided. "It'll save time, and I won't have to walk near as far."

"Granny-Bee said those woods aren't safe. They might even be *haunted.*"

"Are you scared of her stupid old stories?" his twin challenged.

"I guess not. But what if we get lost?"

"How could we do that? We keep the sun at our backs; that's west. Granny-Bee's cottage is due east. Shoot! It's lucky you weren't leading a wagon train to California. You'd have had the poor fools in Mexico or Canada in no time."

He ignored her jibe. After a determining glance at the westering sun, they headed off in the opposite direction, where a deer path seemed to offer a straight-and-true way directly east into the piney woods.

"I wish we hadn't thrown our luck bags away," Kwame said as they entered the green-but-growing-darker shade of the trees.

"I wish you hadn't thrown your brains away," she retorted.

After this, they struggled along in a silence broken only by Kazija's now all-too-real groans and gasps.

Soon the trail began to meander left and right but still seemed pretty much on course. The trees grew thicker and pressed in on them. The clouds above were tinted a cheery red-orange, but shadows were pooling under the pines and oaks. It was becoming harder to see. An occasional misstep made them stumble, and Kazija cried out.

"Granny-Bee is going to raise holy you-know-what when we get back," Kwame said at one point.

"I just want to get back. We can deal with her later." Kazija's voice sounded weak and strained. This disturbed her brother more than the gathering shadows and the uncertain path underfoot. He always looked to his sister as the stronger of them — never mind his occasional loss of temper.

A warm gust of air—as soft as someone's breath—passed over Kwame's face. It tickled, which startled him. He brushed at what he thought was a spider web he had blundered into.

"Why are you stopping?"

"Something's on my face."

She looked carefully, then said, "You're crazy. Come *on!* I want to get out of here before night."

But the boy remained rooted in place. Far ahead, where the shadows deepened as the path dipped through a small depression, he saw a little, black cloud of mist float out of the brush and drift across the trail. "Look at that!" He pointed. Kazija looked but saw nothing. The mist vanished into the trees as quickly as it had appeared. So brief was his glimpse, Kwame was no longer sure he had seen anything.

They moved forward. The boy, on the alert, saw nothing more. But when they crossed the spot where he thought he had seen the cloud, he smelled something foul. The stink seemed to clog in his nostrils and catch at the back of his throat.

"*Eeewww!*" his sister said, wrinkling her nose. "Something died around here."

They continued on as quickly as her injury would allow, but the stench followed them, clinging to their skin and clothing.

As they climbed the path up the far side of the hollow, Kwame got the sensation that something was following them. The hair at the back of his neck prickled. He could almost feel a pair of eyes boring like hot pins into his back. But though he turned around several times, he couldn't spy anything. He again found himself regretting the thoughtless way they had disposed of Granny-Bee's luck bags. "Can you go any faster?" he asked, unable to keep the anxiety out of his voice.

"I can't," she answered, sounding close to tears. Her fear and frustration were all too clear to her twin.

The path suddenly cut sharply left. "This doesn't look good," Kwame muttered. But he didn't dare slow down, and retracing their steps through the stinking, haunted hollow was unthinkable.

Here the trees bore heavier burdens of Spanish moss, dangling like hanks of gray hair or strands of solidified smoke. In the twilight, the stuff seemed to glow with pale light. Above, the clouds had darkened to bluish-purple in a sky now black enough to reveal a scattering of the brightest stars. They had to slow down to avoid tripping over rocks and roots.

At one point, Kazija suddenly gasped and stumbled.

"Did you catch your foot?" her brother asked.

She shook her head. "I'm just too tired, and my ankle's gotten worse. I've got to sit down." She ignored his protests and found a fallen log to sit on, lowering herself with the help of the walking stick. Admitting his own weariness, Kwame dropped down beside her. But he kept watch on the trail behind them. Some inner alarm was warning him that this was the direction from which any danger would come.

Around them, twilight came alive with familiar wood-land noises: chirring crickets, a calling owl, harumphing bullfrogs on some unseen pond.

Then the dusk fell unnaturally silent.

"Look up," whispered his sister, so softly he hardly heard her.

Reluctant to take his eyes off the path for even a moment, Kwame followed her raised finger. Just above a stand of tall pines, the sliver of a new moon was visible.

"Spirits walk in the night when the moon is young," said his sister, fear making her words even fainter. "That's what Granny-Bee said." To Kwame, she sounded like a weary, frightened little girl, not the self-assured Kazija he knew.

"You don't believe that stuff," he said, managing to sound far more positive than he felt. "I sure don't." But he did. He was watching the path every minute.

"You're lying," she said without resentment. "You're just trying to make me feel better." She grabbed her make-shift crutch with one hand and leaned on his shoulder with the other. "Let's get moving. There's still light enough to see the path."

He helped steady her on her feet, but her fingers sud-denly dug into his shoulder, and she groaned.

"Ouch! Take it easy! I'm sorry if I hurt you," he gasped.

She just continued to moan. Then he saw that it wasn't the pain in her foot that distressed her. Her eyes were locked on a point about twenty-five feet back along the path. He looked, too. There was something in the middle of the path: a small, black, crouched shape.

Relief flooded Kwame. "It's only a cat."

"No cat has eyes like that."

Then he could see what frightened her. The cat's eyes were as red as two burning coals. Instinctively, the boy took a step backward, putting his arm protectively around his sister to help support her as they retreated. Neither one dared to take his or her eyes off the strange cat.

The creature watched them for a second, then rose up on its hind legs and pawed the air. Still standing in a curiously human way, it took a step toward them. When the boy and the girl moved another step back, the cat advanced a step. It was pacing them, Kwame realized. The animal's jaws split into a mocking grin. With a hiss and a snarl, it suddenly leaped at the children. Kwame reacted by snatching Kazija's walking stick, hurling it spinning at the cat, which seemed to have grown bigger with each step. His aim was true, but the branch whirled harmlessly through the creature's chest, as though the burning-eyed beast were made of nothing more than mist. The crutch *thonked* into a tree trunk five feet farther along the trail.

But the thing was now changing, dissolving into a dark, vapory cloud that swirled like a small cyclone. Impossibly, the red eyes stayed in place at the center of the churning blackness.

The cloud expanded, then began to take on another form. In his mind, Kwame heard his grandmother warning, *That plat-eye can take any shape it wants.* As the twins

watched, half-hypnotized by the unwavering eyes that seemed to bore red-hot into their brains, the smoky stuff shaped itself into a huge hog with steam curling up from the corners of its blood-red eyes. It made no move toward them—just gave a wicked grin.

Then the demon hog was gone, and in the middle of the path stood a six-legged calf, with the same blazing eyes. It reminded Kwame of a spider, and he hated spiders. Once Kazija had put a spider down the back of his shirt, and he had nearly gone crazy before his father had fished it out. His horror at the sight in front of them propelled him to action. He tightened his hold on his sister and told her, "Lean on me as much as you have to. We've got to go *now!*"

"I can't—" she started to say, but he wasn't listening. He swung her around, and the two of them hopped and stumbled and hurried as best they could through the trees. Kwame had the sudden impression that he was playing a life-or-death version of the three-legged race he had run on the last school field day. His sister stopped arguing and did her best to keep up as Kwame half dragged her down the trail.

In his effort to keep them both upright, Kwame didn't dare turn around, but he kept his ears alert for the sound of pursuit. Beside him, Kazija panted and winced and some-how managed to bite back the cries at the pain her injury must be giving her as they stumbled along. The path in front of them was barely more than a pale smear in the faint starlight and the thin glimmer from the young moon.

Hearing nothing, Kwame dared to slow their headlong

flight. While his sister sobbed on his shoulder—from pain, exhaustion, and fear—he risked a look behind them.

"No!" he gasped, nearly out of breath himself. Behind them, no nearer and no farther than the first cat-thing had been, the cloud was swirling into the most terrifying shape yet: the tall, ink-black figure of a man—but a man without a head! Above the stump where the neck ended rose a churning vapor about the size and shape of a human head. It was featureless, except for two big, red eyes that burned into Kwame's own.

"Don't look," he warned his sister. But something of her old spirit had come back. She ignored him and looked full at the monstrosity that regarded them from eyes without a face.

This time it was Kazija who hauled her brother after her. "Run away . . . from it . . . Gran said . . . that's our . . . only hope." Her words puffed out in bursts between gasping for breath and blasts of pain from her foot. Her brother said nothing, putting all his energy into escaping. *But where in these haunted woods is any hope of safety?* he wondered.

Behind them the thing roared with laughter—mirthless laughter from a mouthless head. The sound quickly faded away, swallowed by the darkness. Then there were only the sounds of their desperate flight through the woods.

Abruptly, miraculously, a light appeared amid the trees ahead—a glimmer of butter-yellow hope in the threatening blackness. The path, almost impossible to see, cut left, then right, then left again. The beacon vanished, reappeared, then vanished again.

"Help!" Kwame shouted—amazed he'd found the lung power to emit more than a squeak.

From somewhere up ahead, he heard a familiar voice call back, "Children! That you?"

"Granny-Bee!" he answered. "I'm here! Kazija's hurt! Plat-eye's after us!"

"Follow my voice and follow the light," their grandmother shouted. "I'll keep talking; you just keep moving. If it's the plat-eye, you don't dare stop!"

She kept calling to them. The path twisted and turned. But the youngsters caught enough glimpses of the old woman's light to feel growing hope. As near as Kwame could guess, the old plat-eye had abandoned the chase.

Then, where the barely visible trail rounded the bole of an immense oak, they discovered Granny-Bee standing in the middle of the path, her old-fashioned oil lantern held high and her face a mask of mingled concern and care.

The twins stumbled into the welcoming circle of light. The old woman's arms wrapped themselves around the children's shoulders, hugging them to her.

"How did you know where to find us?" asked Kwame.

"I've been searchin' and searchin'," she said. "Somethin' told me you children would wind up just where I told you not t'go."

Kwame barely heard her. He was looking all around for signs of the plat-eye.

"Don't worry," his grandmother said. "Plat-eye isn't out there anymore."

"How can you be sure?"

"I feel it in my bones. You don't live in these parts as long as I have without learnin' some things. But maybe now you two'll pay attention when your elders tell you things."

"We're sorry," Kwame assured her. "But Kazija's foot is hurt. We need to get her home. Maybe to a doctor."

"Come along, then," the woman said, supporting Kazija on one side while Kwame took her other. "It's not far."

But the path seemed to go on forever. Kwame kept searching for telltale lights that would signal Granny-Bee's cottage. But the woods seemed to unfold endlessly all around, lit only by the faint light of the young moon that had now risen to its highest point in the sky. The boy was grateful for the soothing yellow glow from the lantern. Still, he couldn't help asking, "Are you sure we're going the right way?"

"Do you know a better way?" asked Granny-Bee with a grin. Her arm tightened around Kazija. The girl, who had been mostly carried along by her brother and her grandmother, and who appeared to Kwame to have fallen into a walking sleep, gave a weak protest and tried to shift free of the old woman's hold.

"Plat-eye can take any shape, can't it?" said Kwame, stopping suddenly.

"Granny-Bee said so," said Kazija, drifting into the conversation.

"Yes," their grandmother said. "I recall saying something like that."

"Not *you*, our *real* Granny-Bee!" Kwame said. He didn't have to look past his sister's frightened face to know that the old woman's eyes were turning as red as the lantern light that was no longer yellow, but glowing the color of blood.

tour de force

"**R**emember, not one word about this to *anyone*," Sam Wells warned his younger brother, Ethan, and Ethan's best friend, Jacob Hooper.

The eleven-year-olds in the backseat made faces at each other. "Yeah, yeah!" said Ethan. "We know the drill. We're all going to a Scooby-Doo flick."

"I saw that look, bro," said Sam. "We'll all be so busted if Mom and Dad find out I took you weenies to the Tour de Force concert instead of the movies."

"We paid for our tickets ourselves," Ethan protested.

His brother sighed.

"This is going to be so cool," said Paul Alpers, Sam's friend, the other front-seat passenger, paying no attention to the brotherly bickering. "Forcemeat is going to be there. Vendetta. Entropy Means." He ticked off the groups on his fingertips. "But none of them compare to The Mind Parasites. Man! To get to meet them up close and per-sonal—I still can't believe you scored a pair of backstage passes, Sammy-whammy!"

"It's all who you know," said Sam smugly. "I told you that Mike Kriss is working for his dad's newspaper this summer, and he's always getting freebies like this."

"Nice if he could have gotten two more," grumbled Ethan.

"Shut up, brat!" his brother warned. "I'm already sorry I dragged you losers along." He guided his car into a spot on the gravel parking area outside the county fairgrounds. The lot was two-thirds full. Big-amped music from one of the opening bands roared past the cyclone fence surround-ing the scattered concession tents and stage areas. The foursome climbed out of the car and headed for the gate. When they had surrendered their tickets, Sam turned to Ethan and Jacob and said, "Be back here at eleven, sharp. That will give us time to see The Mind Parasites, groove with them a little backstage, and still get us home in time enough to keep things cool."

"Come on," urged Paul. "I wanna check out some of the stages and see a few of the other bands."

"Lose yourselves until eleven. Then be back here or you are so much dead meat," said Sam.

"Thanks," said Ethan. "You have a great time, too!" The younger boys stood side by side, watching the older ones swallowed up by the crowds milling around the half-dozen stages and tents that offered everything from CDs and DVDs by the Tour de Force groups to T-shirts and tofu burgers.

Ethan watched until he was sure his brother and Paul were well out of sight. Then he reached into his pocket and pulled out two bright red tickets.

"Ta-da!" he said. "Look what I scored."

"What are those?" Jacob asked.

"Backstage passes to meet The Mind Parasites—*up close and personal,* like my brother said."

"Do you know that newspaper guy?"

"No. I slipped these out of Sam's wallet two hours ago. He's going to think he lost them."

"If he finds out . . ."

"I've been to concerts before. If you don't have a pass, there's no way they'll let you anywhere near backstage. We'll be fine. Sam won't find out—unless you blab. And I don't think you're that dumb, no matter how stupid you look." Ethan gave his friend a companionable shove. "Let's go get a burger—a real one, not that tofu stuff."

By the time the public-address system announced, "The Mind Parasites now appearing in the main tent," the boys had blown several weeks' worth of allowances on burgers, nachos, sodas, and cotton candy—most of which they wound up pushing into each other's faces. Laughing and pulling the pink spun sugar off their faces, they joined the crowd flowing into the central red-and-white-striped tent.

"Keep an eye out for Sam and Paul," Ethan warned. "I don't want them to see us. By now my brother's probably missed his passes. I'm hoping he thinks he lost them. We'll just say we watched the show, then went to one of the food tents."

Jacob nodded, not really listening, all his attention focused on the stage at the far end of the jammed tent. The stage went dark. The audience was suddenly silent.

Then The Mind Parasites were there: Colin McCambridge, lead guitar; Mercedes Black, vocalist; Trey and Ian Connors, second guitar and drums—a swirl of black leather, black-rimmed eyes, multicolored hair, glinting nose, lip, eyebrow, and ear studs and rings—all flickering under strobe lights. The band was amped to the max. The crowd roared. Jacob made a face and clapped his hands to his ears. Ethan laughed and mouthed, "You wuss!" His words and laughter were drowned by the clash of the music and the clamorous response of the audience.

Occasionally Ethan scanned the crowd for signs of his brother or Paul, but he saw only a sea of bobbing heads in a forest of waving arms. He let the wild music carry him to the places the lyrics described as "black waste space behind the stars" or "abysmal pits that even devils don't dare stare into" or "the nightmare realm beyond Elm Street." The words and music—familiar from CDs Ethan's parents didn't suspect he had downloaded onto his iPod—sounded stunningly fresh and powerful, spinning him off on a chilling, thrilling, hypnotic mind trip. Jacob, the crowd, everything around him became a background blur to the experience. There were only the wailing vocals; leaping, gyrating performers; and the wave on wave of shrill, throbbing, ear-and-brain-blasting music washing over the hyped-up audience.

Triple-Dare to Be Scared

The music has a dark power inside, Ethan suddenly thought. Only the merest hint of it came across in recordings. Live—*here, now*—the music seemed to boil through his head, connect with every nerve in his body, leave him an empty shell adrift on a storm-lashed sea that was churning faster and faster—becoming a vast whirlpool that would draw him down into the "black waste space" the band sang about to pulsing guitars and relentless drumming. He sang, shouted, screamed along with the pulsating music.

Beside him, Jacob was rocking and writhing, captive to the music—just like Ethan—just like everyone in the tent. There was nothing but the music and the musicians.

Then it was over. The music cut off as sharply as if sliced off. No encores, no return to the stage to acknowledge the hysterical shouts of their fans—nothing but the four performers marching offstage, without a backward glance, job done. Behind them, the fanatic, frantic audience screamed, begged for more, one more taste of heavy-metal mental mayhem.

Still half-dazed, Ethan grabbed Jacob's arm. "Now we go backstage!" he said. It hurt him to talk. His throat had been scraped raw by all the shouting and screaming the music had wrenched out of him. Jacob still seemed to be coming down from the music himself. He nodded vaguely and let his friend tug him along through the lingerers who were hoping to force an encore by rhythmic clapping and determined waiting. But Ethan knew enough about the group to know they never returned for an encore, no matter how loudly their audience demanded or begged for more.

"Shoot!" whispered Ethan. "There's Sam. I don't think he's seen us, but we've got to get out of here fast!"

Jacob caught the urgency in Ethan's voice. The boys shoved their way through the glut of people who had finally gotten the message that the show was over and were now slowly exiting the tent. A few people yelled at them or shoved back, but they cleared the entrance well before Sam reached it.

They ducked around the tent to the back, where three trailers were lined up. It was easy to spot the one belonging to The Mind Parasites; their logo was emblazoned all over — something with spread wings like a bat, but with a demon's head, was feasting on the top of a grinning skull. It was stamped on all the group's CDs. There was no sign of The Mind Parasites themselves. Thirty feet from their trailer, the boys were stopped by one of the security guards. But when Ethan pulled out the two passes, the guard grunted and nodded toward a group that was gathering in a small, roped-off area. Everyone seemed to be carrying blood-red passes. The boys burrowed deep into the middle of the crowd. Someone complained to one of the guards, "Hey, man! We've got passes!"

"Passes get you this far," the guard said. "The group doesn't let everyone into their trailer; they'll make a choice. So hold your water."

More people joined the mix. Jacob suddenly elbowed Ethan in the ribs, nodding to where Ethan's brother and his friend were approaching them. Screened by the outer ring of fans in the holding area, Ethan watched as Sam and Paul talked to the guards—clearly trying to convince them that they should be allowed in. The guards weren't buying, and the two were turned away. Ethan could see that his brother was frustrated and furious; Paul was clearly trying to calm his buddy down. Ethan didn't want to think what would happen if Sam found out he had lifted the passes. He felt he could carry off the deception, but he was growing worried that Jacob might fold under questioning and blurt out everything. Ethan was going to have to make very sure the other boy understood just how much was at stake. Ethan had experienced Sam's anger, and it wasn't pretty.

Then a ripple ran through the crowd. The Mind Parasites' lead guitarist, Colin McCambridge, had stepped down from the band's trailer and was sauntering toward the group waiting behind the ropes and stanchions. The muttering, complaining voices grew suddenly quiet. It seemed to Ethan that everyone was equally eager and uncomfortable as Colin's mascara-ringed eyes raked them one at a time.

Stuck in the middle of the crowd, Ethan despaired that he and his friend would even be spotted. But Colin circled the group twice, flanked by two rent-a-cops, then suddenly pointed at Ethan and Jacob. Those around them protested as the guards beckoned the boys to step beyond the ropes.

"You're the lucky ones," said the taller of the two guards. He put out his hand, and Ethan surrendered their passes. Colin watched without comment, then suddenly turned and headed back to the trailer, motioning with his head to indicate that the boys should follow him. The hopefuls left behind called after Colin and argued with the guards, who listened impassively. "Better luck next time," the shorter guard said to one particularly loud protester.

Ethan, excited by how things had worked out, punched Jacob's shoulder. "We made it! We're in!"

"Yeah," said Jacob in a flat voice, rubbing his shoulder; his enthusiasm seemed to ebb away with each step he took toward the trailer whose windows were shrouded with red curtains behind which candles flickered. An article Ethan had read in a fanzine had mentioned that the group preferred candlelight when coming down from the electric glare onstage.

Colin stepped up to the door, holding it open for the two boys. The guards stopped about five feet away.

"I don't think I want to," said Jacob, holding back.

"Don't wimp out now!" hissed Ethan, putting his foot on the lower metal step up to the trailer door. "I went to a lot of trouble to get these passes. I'm the one Sam is going to pound if he ever figures things out."

With a sigh that turned into a shudder, Jacob nodded bleakly. Then he followed his friend up the two metal steps and into the trailer.

The inside seemed roomier than possible. It was draped with red and black curtains. The light came from a sea of candles shivering in red glass holders. There were no chairs, just pillows. Sitting or sprawling across these were the other three band members: Mercedes Black, who eyed the two boys closely, while the twins, Trey and Ian Connors, intent on adjusting the strings on Trey's guitar, barely glanced up at the newcomers.

"Names," said Colin. To Ethan, the voice was too soft for someone who had just blasted a tentful of people into nightmare spaces beyond the darkest stars. But the word seemed less a question than a command.

Ethan spoke for them both, since Jacob seemed to have lost his voice completely. His friend looked very pale, even in the rosy candlelight.

"Young," said Mercedes. Ethan couldn't tell if she approved or disapproved of Colin's choice of visitors.

"Sit," said Colin.

The boys sat side by side on a single pillow. Colin eased down beside Mercedes and put his arm around her shoulder. The twins stopped tinkering with the guitar and looked across at their young fans, then broke into perfectly matched grins.

"You guys on your own?" asked Mercedes.

"My brother and a friend are somewhere," said Ethan, trying to sound casual. "They're not such big fans as we are."

"Our loss," said either Ian or Trey with a shrug. Without an identifying guitar or drums, Ethan couldn't tell them apart.

"So they'll be looking for you pretty soon," said Mercedes.

"We've got to meet them by eleven," Jacob blurted.

"Time enough," said Colin. He moved to one curtained wall and pulled some of the billowing red cloth aside to reveal what had to be a CD player framed by the weirdest speakers Ethan had ever seen.

"Can we ask you some questions? And get some autographs?" asked Ethan.

"No questions yet," said Ian (or Trey).

"Autographs later," said Trey (or Ian).

"Music now," said Colin, slipping in a CD. "Something you haven't heard before. Something you won't hear again." He smiled.

"Something just for you guys," said Mercedes. Now she was smiling, too. Something about the smiles and the eyes that never seemed to leave the boys—eyes that didn't seem to blink, even—was beginning to creep Ethan out. He glanced sideways at Jacob and saw that his friend looked miserable. He was sweating, too—though the trailer seemed overly air-conditioned.

The music began softly, as though it were coming from far away. Ethan had to strain to hear. It sounded like guitars and drums and someone—Mercedes?—singing. But it was a song composed of strange sounds, no words (at least, no words the boy could understand). Now he could hear more drums and a strange piping, like flutes, and the *cling-clang* of finger cymbals, then the reedy music a synthesizer might make—but playing notes so high they almost hurt his ears. There was no melody that he could make out, no through-line. It was like the record was a sampler of all kinds of music, from technopop through stuff that sounded like American Indian chants and Chinese singing from a kung fu movie and tons of other stuff all jumbled and jangled together. Every moment it was growing louder, now hurting his ears in fact, beginning to fill his head with not pictures but shapes, patterns, static—with a vague impression of yawning depths and vastness beyond. Gradually, a strange vision formed in his mind: a pitch-black landscape under a red sun, unending strangeness filled with distorted, moving shapes that crawled, loped, scuttled, and flew. "I see Nightmare Alley," Ethan said. He strained to understand the meaning in the music and the images that were in some crazy way the same thing.

"*Sssshhh!*" said Colin, raising a finger elaborately to his smiling lips. "Listen."

"Lose yourself in the music," Mercedes said. And that was easy to do. The impact on Ethan was like the effect of the music earlier—only ratcheted up a hundred—a *thousand*—times. He felt utterly helpless in its grip.

"I want to go now," begged Jacob. To Ethan, he sounded tired and cranky, like a child up past his bedtime. *Pathetic.* "Please, I want to *go*."

"Not just yet," said one of the twins. Or were they both speaking together? Ethan wondered. Things were getting blurry. He rubbed his eyes. The space seemed to be darkening, the fluttering red interior deepening to black. The music was filling the room and his head. Beside him, Jacob sighed deeply, then softly collapsed onto the cushion like a deflated balloon. The air he had breathed out rushed past Ethan, tickling his right ear and cheek. In his increasingly smeary vision that no amount of eye rubbing would help, he could swear that he saw Jacob's sigh as a faint, red-tinted haze that twisted across the room like the intertwined tendrils of the passion vine that grew on the back fence at home.

As he stared, uncertainly but fascinated, the sigh-vine began to unravel into four misty strands. The four figures across the room, now little more than vague shadows in the thickening darkness, inhaled deeply, drinking in the red breath. Unable to look away from the others, Ethan reached for Jacob's hand and felt something soft and feathery that abruptly fell apart in his grip, like the ashes from a rolled-up newspaper that had been burned ages ago. Numbly he looked down at his hand. Something like faint red soot clung to his fingers and palm, then vanished even as he watched.

"What?" he asked, unable to utter more than that single word.

"Lost in the music," said someone. He couldn't tell which of the shadows had spoken.

"Who are . . . ?" The rest of Ethan's question caught in his throat.

"Musicians," said another voice. "From *very* far away."

"We live through the music," added a third.

"We live *because* of the music," a fourth voice corrected. Or was it four voices in one? "Where we come from, what you call 'music' is simply a by-product of energies that let us lure in our prey and transfer that being's vital energies directly to us. We feast—but in a way you can't imagine. On other worlds, the energy by-product is *color* that draws a victim to us. That being's life force comes to us in a rush of color. *Delicious.*"

"You guys are"—he searched for the right word in a mind grown confused and uncertain, found it, and said—"*hunters.*"

"Exactly," said the voice (or voices).

"Why . . . us?"

"Something a little . . . different . . . from the usual fans or groupies or occasional roadies who come our way."

"My brother . . ." Ethan said.

"Yes, well, he'll have a lot of explaining to do. People will want to know why you two boys have run away. But it happens all the time."

"People saw us outside," said Ethan, the muscles in his throat as weak as the muscles in his arms and legs now. It was an effort to get the four words out.

"Things are confused when there are crowds," said a voice that seemed mostly Mercedes' but was threaded with the others' voices, too. "Our music has that effect. Different impressions on every mind. People will tell fifty different stories, and each one will think he or she is telling the truth. Some might remember you. Most won't. People come and go, and no one notices. Bands come and go. Two days from now, we'll leave this tour and join another. You'll leave very little trace, which will grow less with each passing hour."

Ethan felt weaker still. And cold. He sank back into the thick cushions, hoping he would find warmth in their softness. But he found only a deeper, hungry coldness.

"You . . . can't . . ." But he no longer remembered what he wanted to say. He just wanted to bury himself in the softness beneath him. The cold no longer mattered.

The music was everywhere, and he let himself collapse into it. Inside him and outside him, there was only the music. He was lost in it, unable to resist its hypnotic power. He could make out a few of the sounds now, even though they were nothing like words.

"Welcome to Nightmare Alley," echoed in his brain.

The pillows embraced him as he crumpled down.

He sighed deeply and watched helplessly, vaguely, regretfully, as his last breath snaked redly across the room toward the hungry, eager darkness that was four in one.

In seconds, the crimson residue on the cushions faded to ash gray, then disappeared altogether.

underwater

Owen Henderson hated the whole idea of being underwater. He avoided going to the pool with friends. He could not watch a movie in a theater or on DVD if it had any underwater scenes. He would leave the room, visit the snack counter, or simply refuse to go. Ancient films like *Creature from the Black Lagoon* or the original *Godzilla* bothered him as much as more recent DVDs like *The Abyss* or even *Finding Nemo*. As soon as the view dipped below the surface of the river, lake, or ocean, he was out of there.

His adoptive parents wondered if it had something to do with his being found abandoned on the edge of Green Lake near the Bighorn Mountains of Wyoming. The small, still lake took its name from the waterweed that clogged it and gave it a deep, emerald color; layer after layer floated over sunless depths.

When the boy, who looked to be about three years old, was discovered by campers, it was at first assumed his parents had been drowned in an accident. The lake was notorious for reports of duck hunters and swimmers being pulled under the water, never to rise. Most people blamed it on the tangle of waterweed swirling below the surface. But stories persisted that something else lurked in the green-black depths—maybe several somethings.

As proof, some folks pointed out a curious, often-repeated event. Lakes are few and far between in this part of Wyoming. Every year, thousands of wild ducks settled on the lake to spend the night as they winged their way from Canada down across the Rockies in their annual migration. Many times hunters and fishermen swore they had seen the ducks suddenly rise off the lake, their ten thousand wings beating frantically with a feathery roar in an astonishing spectacle.

From this grew the story that the fowl were frightened by a monstrous aquatic serpent—or pair of them—with huge jaws and shining teeth. These (it was said) would suddenly shoot to the surface, snatch mouthfuls of slower-escaping ducks, then sink back into the green murk. Some lake visitors claimed to have glimpsed the creatures, though their brief appearances were curtained by the welter of flapping wings from wave upon wave of terrified, skyborne waterfowl.

Such tales were largely dismissed as just one more

puzzle linked to the small, isolated lake. The mystery of Owen Henderson was the most recent. There was no clue as to how he had wound up in such a lonely place — no clue as to parents or guardians. Searchers had expected to find an abandoned camp, which would have indicated a parent or parents lost to a drowning or some other wilderness accident. But nothing was found that hinted at the child's identity. He had a rich, golden tone to his skin, and his eyes were slightly almond-shaped, which suggested possibly Eurasian parentage. The child himself had no helpful memories. He recalled nothing earlier than the moment two duck hunters, on their way to a blind, had found him — a naked toddler playing in the mucky lake mud, fashioning curious shapes that suggested the letters of some weird language. He had no grasp of English, speaking only a meaningless mishmash of sounds. At first he was diagnosed as mildly autistic, but he quickly revealed an amazing capacity for learning and was soon on par with — then ahead of — children his age when he started school.

Placed at first in foster homes, he was adopted just short of his estimated fifth birthday by a childless couple, Max and Nancy Henderson, who lived in Laramie. His parents gave him all the love they could, but Owen, though polite and obedient and (on the surface) affectionate, always seemed distant in his mind from his parents. He felt their disappointment, their sense of having failed him somehow. *He* sensed he had failed *them*. The distance grew, in spite of his parents' attempts to pull him closer. He made

a real effort to love them, but he knew, deep inside, that he was only pretending. As he grew older, he asked endlessly about his real parents. The honest answer — "Nobody knows" — only frustrated him and pushed them all farther apart. When his sister, Amilee, was born, Owen felt more than ever like a visitor in the household. The trip to Green Lake was the latest attempt to draw Owen more fully into the family circle.

By the time he was twelve, he seemed normal — an above-average student, a child who was not troublesome, but remained a bit shy and standoffish, and often seemed to his parents to be miles away in his mind.

Only his fear of water and his frequent nightmares of drowning, beginning in what was declared his seventh year, upset his parents. They took him to doctors and counselors, who offered numerous (and often contradictory) explanations: he was experiencing a delayed reaction to the loss of his birth parents or he had been frightened by something he had seen in Green Lake or maybe he had almost drowned in its waters before he had been found, and so on. Nothing helped; his fear of water persisted.

Max Henderson, Owen's adoptive father, was an avid duck hunter. He would often go to Green Lake with his buddies. For years, he never made an effort to bring his son along. But shortly after Owen's twelfth birthday (the date in late March when his adoption had become finalized), Max suggested — *insisted* — that the boy accompany him to the lake.

Nancy Henderson protested, "That place has bad memories for him. Who knows what this might stir up?"

But Max, who was usually easygoing, had made up his mind that this adventure would serve a double purpose: it would be a father-son bonding experience (since the "glue" binding the boy to the rest of the family seemed to be weakening with every passing day), and more importantly, it would prove to his son (who cringed at any mention of Green Lake) that there was nothing frightening about the body of water—as long as a person followed basic safety rules.

Owen said simply, "I don't want to go."

"We're going, and that's that," his father said.

Owen glanced at his mother, but she just shrugged her shoulders and said, "It's important to your father. I think you should go."

The boy tried a temper tantrum—arguing loudly and locking himself in his room behind a slammed door. But this only made his father more stubborn. His mother took him aside and pleaded, "Do it for my sake. It's not so much to ask: Friday and Saturday nights, and you'll be home Sunday afternoon." He gave in.

So they rode up to the lake Friday afternoon in the backseat of Marty Dracott's SUV, along with John Graf and Stu Quinn. The three were his father's closest friends and avid duck hunters.

Owen had to admit that the lake, like a gem in a setting of reeds and scrub, looked pretty innocent. In the light of the westering sun, it appeared red-gold instead of green. The surface was a mass of ducks, calmly settling in for the night. But as the SUV rounded the last turn and came to a stop on the gravel-strewn parking area beside the water, his breathing became shorter, and his palms and armpits grew sweaty, though the evening breeze had a chill to it.

Sensing his son's unease, Max put a hand on his shoulder. "Easy, big guy." Owen shrugged off the comforting hand, not wanting the men in the two forward seats to realize how frightened he was. He wondered if his father had alerted the others to his hang-up and hoped he had not.

"We can put our tents by that picnic table and barbecue pit," Stu said. The others agreed with his suggestion and set to work pitching tents and pulling out steaks and corn on the cob for roasting. Up and down the shore, Owen could see the campfires and lanterns of hunters' camps. It was comforting to know that so many were within shouting distance. But he sat with his back to the darkening waters, focusing his attention on the distant Bighorn Mountains. The food was good—Max loved to barbecue—and Owen began to think that the weekend wouldn't be too bad. But he was never so lulled into a feeling of well-being that he wasn't aware of the constant splash of lake water against the stones and mud of the shore. It seemed to grow louder as the sounds of the ducks lessened and the darkness (the night was nearly moonless) compressed the points of light marking other campsites to mere pinpricks of brightness.

Owen shared a tent with his father. Stu and John bunked together. Marty pitched his own pup tent a little ways from the others, saying, "You'll appreciate not having to listen to my snoring." Owen had hoped to read a chapter or two of a fantasy novel he had brought along, *The Thief Lord*, but his father said, "Big day tomorrow. We've got to be up early. You'll need your sleep." Max extinguished the Coleman lantern and quickly drifted off, softly snoring.

For a long time Owen stared at the sloping canvas above him. He was used to falling asleep while reading — often in midsentence — with his bedside lamp still on. Now sleep seemed far away. He was aware of the sound of waterfowl, of bugs droning and crickets chirring and frogs calling one another and, more than anything else, of the *splash, splash, splash* of waves on the shore.

In the end, the rhythmic splashing lulled him to sleep, then invaded his dreams. He imagined himself floating on his back on the surface of Green Lake. As the rippling water gently rocked him, the distant camp lights on the circling shore dipped and bobbed like fireflies. For a moment, he felt at peace with his surroundings.

Then he felt his limbs growing chill and heavy, becoming waterlogged. In a panic, he began to thrash about — less afraid of drowning than of being underwater. But his struggles were useless: his increasingly leaden body would not stay afloat. Helplessly he sank into the murky green, which turned swiftly black, as though someone were emptying vast quantities of ink into it. It was all the more horrifying because he could see nothing — just an expanse of emptiness that was far more terrifying than any monster. He tried to shut his eyes, but the dream wouldn't let him. He kept his mouth closed against drowning, but at last he had to open his mouth to gasp for breath, expecting a rush of chilling, suffocating water into his lungs. Instead, he found the experience no different from breathing air. But this gave him no comfort. His body was numb except for a growing sense of horror and hopelessness as he felt himself being pulled deeper.

Now the watery immensity stretched way above, below, and on all sides. He had never felt so alone. He wrapped his arms around himself and drew his legs up to his chest. He imagined himself an infant falling and shrinking into a liquid nightmare grown vaster than an ocean, vaster than the black spaces between the stars.

And then, far below, in the depths, something flickered — silver, long, shining with its own light, since there was nothing but absolute blackness around it. Owen felt a new thrill of fear; if he could have, he would have folded even more tightly into himself.

Another flicker. *Nearer.*

He tried to shout, but the black water of his dream swallowed every sound; it was like shouting into a mass of damp cotton. Suddenly, below, the two lengths of silver crisscrossed, wound around each other, began rising in a whirlpool of light toward him. In the combined glow, he could see two long heads, each split by a mouth filled with eel-like teeth. Much worse were the eyes: dead-black, like the eyes of a shark.

The creatures rushed up at him, and this time his efforts to scream broke through the wet-cotton barrier, ripped through the fabric of his nightmare, and he awoke, shouting his lungs out, while his father tried to calm him. Outside the voices of the other men could be heard, confused, worried, demanding to know what was going on.

"Easy, champ," Max soothed him. "You were having one heck of a nightmare." He sounded, for the first time, uncertain about the wisdom of dragging his son along to Green Lake. But Owen was so drained by his nightmare, he couldn't muster any "I told you so" satisfaction.

His father asked what he had dreamed, but the boy couldn't answer. He just leaned against Max, trembling. It was a little after sunrise, so the other men decided to get a head start on the day. Owen, insisting he was feeling better, told his father to join them.

The morning sun was reflecting brightly off the surface of Green Lake. Stu, wiping sweat off his face as he stirred a pot of instant oatmeal on the kerosene stove, announced, "It's gonna be a warm one." But Owen couldn't get warm. Huddled inside his down jacket, he couldn't shake off the chill that he had felt watching those twin monstrosities spinning up out of the blackness toward him in his dream.

The boy wasn't really hungry, but he appreciated the warmth of the oatmeal and cocoa. He didn't want to wait with the others in the duck blind they planned to set up a quarter-mile from the camp. Max wasn't too happy about leaving him, but his son said he didn't feel up to the trek. He wanted to stay and read. In fact, he had no real interest in hunting; it saddened him to see beautiful creatures like ducks and geese brought down with shotguns and stored in coolers, their next stop the dinner table. He was already deep in the world of *The Thief Lord* when the men set out in their green-brown camouflage outfits and waders, carrying two portable layout blinds they would cover with brush. Then they would lie in wait for their decoys to bring unlucky ducks within range.

Sitting as far from the water as he could (but still in sight of the camp), Owen settled in for a long day. Occasionally he heard the faint popping reports of hunters' guns, but he couldn't tell from what direction they came. After an hour or so, he went back to the camp and rummaged out a bag of SunChips and a can of Pepsi. He also put an extra sweater on under his jacket, then returned to lean against the log that provided him a backrest.

Something was humming over the lake. He tried, at first, to ignore it, but he couldn't resist turning to look. His initial impression was that the sound came from the insects swarming in clouds over the lake. But then he realized the *thrum* was too loud—and almost like music.

The water along the shore seemed stirred up. But out at the lake's center, it was dead calm. He thought of how the eye of a hurricane remained calm at the heart of a raging storm.

Something flashed silver in the midst of the still water. Intrigued, Owen edged closer to the shore. There was a second flicker—hard to make out through the swarming insects and heat shimmers rising off the water.

Curiosity overcoming his reluctance, he edged closer yet. Now he was almost to the lake's edge, where waves slapped the shore. Part of him was surprised and scared at his daring, but another part kept nudging him forward.

He had almost reached the water's margin—nearer than he had ever intended to come. More flicker-flashes blinked far out on the surface. He shaded his eyes, but the humming, cloying insects were worse than ever, the heat shimmers more distorting, too. Feeling like someone in a dream, he took a step closer, slipped on a wet stone, and pitched forward, hands down, into the muddy shallows. His arms sank almost to his elbows in the muck; his knees sank deep, too.

He moved crablike, trying to push himself backward, free of the mud. But it kept slipping under his hands, seeming to become more liquid by the moment.

Suddenly he saw two thin cords of silver whipping across the lake surface like water snakes he'd seen on the Nature Channel. With a cry, he tried more frantically to scramble backward, but his palms could find no purchase in the muck. His knees sank deeper into the hungry mud.

And then the silvery ropes — twice as thick as a garden hose and pocked with suckers like those on an octopus — slithered across the mud and circled his arms. He couldn't tell which — the cords or the suckers — held him more firmly. But there was a gentleness — no pain. Then he was tugged free of the mud with a wet sucking sound. Owen found his voice; he began shouting for help as the tentacles hauled him across the last stretch of mud and into the water. From somewhere far up the shore — he couldn't twist enough to see where — he heard his father and the others shouting. They had returned from the blinds just in time to see him caught. For a moment it seemed weirdly fitting: his dad had bagged ducks, and now something had bagged his son. Then Owen's hands were pulled into the lake. His shouts turned to screams that were cut off as the water closed over him and he was drawn down and away from the shore. The lake depths were a confusion of green-brown-gray-black ripples and shadows through which he plummeted.

He tried to keep his mouth clamped shut to avoid drowning, but it was impossible. He opened it with a cry that erupted as a gurgle of bubbles racing for the surface as he was hauled down and down. Water flooded his mouth, nose, lungs. He struggled furiously, but the silver bonds drew him relentlessly toward the blurry darkness that, he realized, was the secret heart of the lake.

Then he became aware of something totally unexpected: the water in his lungs wasn't choking him. It felt normal; his lungs seemed to be working all right, pulling air from water with the same unstudied ease his lungs pulled in everyday air. *Just like in my dream,* he thought wonderingly.

Fear shook him again. I must be drowning, he decided. He remembered his friend Jamie, who had almost drowned in the deep end of the community pool, saying that he felt spacey and calm just before the lifeguard pulled him out. But though he was breathing—or something like it—Owen didn't feel calm. He still struggled against the silver cords; his fear was growing as he sank into the depths, a place only hinted at in his worst nightmares. His imagination filled with pictures: his father and friends inflating the rubber raft they had brought and paddling back and forth above, hopelessly searching for him, then calling emergency services. Helicopters darting like dragonflies over the lake. Reports on the six and ten o'clock news. His mother crying. His little sister crying, too, without really understanding why.

Hopeless. Hopeless.

The water became darker as he descended. *How deep am I?* Owen wondered. Still his lungs functioned. He thought of Tom Hanks following the mermaid into the ocean in the movie *Splash.* He thought of the guy in *The Abyss* breathing that special brown stuff that flooded his diving suit and let him go deeper into the ocean than anyone had ever gone. Both were movies he hadn't been able to watch but had made his friends at school describe for him.

His eyes seemed to be adjusting more slowly than his lungs to the water, but things were getting clearer. He could see his hands, see the suckers on the tentacles pulsing slowly, clearly alive. What had caught him? Where was it taking him? Why? All he could distinguish were the two cords pulling him down.

He imagined some awful deepwater monster — all mouth and teeth and hunger reeling him in. He tried to break free again and again but failed every time.

In despair, he surrendered to the downward drag.

Far below — just as in his nightmare — something silver flashed from side to side. An instant later, a second something flickered in the opposite direction. Owen had the impression that the cords binding him disappeared into the darkness where — *flash, flicker* — the things waited, impatiently. He was so overwhelmed by the horror of being so far, so hopelessly underwater, that nothing seemed to matter. He was dully aware of the silver ropes binding him, the flashing shapes, the certainty of becoming a monster-fish's dinner.

Down where the water was utterly black, the two lengths of living silver circled each other like dancers, then became spirals winding around each other, swirling up toward him. Now he could see that the silver cords emerged from the foreheads of two snakelike creatures. They had fivefold eyes that sparkled—black as sharks' eyes—but with an eagerness and a longing nothing like sharks' deadly hunger.

They had stopped their spiraling dance and were now gazing up, as the cords pulled him nearer. But the eyes regarding him seemed somehow gentle. *Are you thinking you'll find mercy here?* some part of his brain mocked. *You're delirious. You're dying.*

A memory fragment bubbled up—his father raising a glass to his lips, reciting:

> *"Over the lips,*
> *Through the gums—*
> *Look out stomach,*
> *Here it comes."*

Suddenly, when he was still a distance above the creatures, the tentacles released him, retreating into the silver foreheads. The fish-scale skin rippled a moment, then smoothed itself on each head.

Freed, Owen turned and fumbled toward the surface, not so much swimming as scrambling like a rock climber.

Then he relaxed his efforts as he felt his body flood with a sensation of well-being, tenderness, and welcoming. Proof of drowning, he wondered, or . . . something else?

There was a noise in his head like the earlier *thrum* over the lake that had caught his interest. This time the vague humming hardened into words in his mind. He was aware of two voices. STOP, commanded one. WAIT, said a softer, pleading one.

Who are you? What do you want? he tried to ask, unable to force the words from his mind into his water-clogged lungs.

THINK THE WORDS, said the softer "voice"—DON'T USE YOUR VOICE BOX. IT IS USELESS HERE.

So he formed the question in his mind. *What – who – are you?*

FATHER, said the first voice; MOTHER, echoed the gentler one.

The answers stunned him, yet somehow he felt there was a rightness to the words.

WE WERE SENT FROM OUR HOMEWORLD AS PART OF OUR ONGOING OBSERVATION OF THIS WORLD. BUT OUR SHIP MALFUNCTIONED ON APPROACH. WE WERE PROGRAMMED FOR ANOTHER AREA BUT CRASH-LANDED HERE IN THE ONLY AVAILABLE WATER, WHICH HIDES US AND PROVIDES AN ENVIRONMENT MOST LIKE HOME. DURING THE TIME IT TOOK TO JOURNEY BETWEEN STAR SYSTEMS, YOU WERE BORN. SO MUCH WAS DAMAGED OR DESTROYED ON IMPACT, WE COULD NOT REPROGRAM THE SHIP'S "BRAIN." WE HAD TO WAIT FOR COMMANDS TO BE SENT FROM A WAY STATION LIGHT-YEARS FROM HERE. THE

TRANSMISSION HAS TAKEN A LONG TIME, BUT THE SHIP IS FUNCTIONING AGAIN. YET, BECAUSE THERE WAS A DANGER THE DESTABILIZED SHIP COULD SELF-DESTRUCT—OR THAT WE MIGHT BE FOUND BY THOSE WHO WOULD SEE US AS "INVADERS," WE TOOK STEPS TO ENSURE YOUR SAFETY. THERE IS A DEVICE— (Owen suddenly had the image of a mass of flickers and sounds wrapped around a cocoon of pulsing blue light in which a smaller version of the Father was transformed into . . . a younger Owen.)

(Mother) IF WE DIED, YOU WOULD BE SAFE—ON LAND OR IN WATER. BUT, BECAUSE THE INSTABILITY OF THE SHIP REMAINED A DANGER, WE PROGRAMMED A WARNING IN YOUR BRAIN TO KEEP AWAY FROM THIS PLACE, THE WATER.

So that's where my fear came from, Owen realized.

(Father) BUT WHEN WE REALIZED THE SHIP WAS HEALED AND WE COULD RETURN HOME—

Owen had a sudden vision of coral-reeflike cities, gardens of waving waterweed, and an endless variety of craft glistening like mother-of-pearl as they sped or drifted through shining deeps.

WE SENT OUT A MIND BEACON TO CALL YOU BACK. (Mother)

My nightmares, thought Owen.

BUT THE EARLIER DEEP WARNING CONFUSED OUR MESSAGES. (Father)

Maybe some of it spilled into the mind of my dad – my human dad, Owen wondered. *Maybe that's why he suddenly had to come to Green Lake.*

HOWEVER IT DREW YOU, YOU ARE RETURNED TO US. AND WE MUST SOON DEPART. (Mother)

He thought of his life. His adoptive parents. He knew they would be saddened, thinking him drowned. But they still had Amilee. And he had never felt a part of them, truly. He had always felt he belonged somewhere else. Feelings he had never been able to share with Max and Nancy began to well up in him.

He let his growing happiness wash away the last of his sadness.

Then the three swam down. Below he could see the ship glowing like a pearl. And the heart of darkness no longer held nightmares: it held promise.

far site

"**N**erd!" Matt said with a grin.

"Geek!" Nikolai countered with a matching smile.

It was the first day of classes at Saint Michael's Catholic School. The two fourth graders had met in the far corner of the schoolyard, on a green-painted wooden bench with black cast-iron armrests and legs. Above them, crowning the slope covered with purple-flowered ice plant, loomed a huge, weathered white statue of the archangel Michael, the school's patron. The tip of one wing was broken off, but the span remained impressive. And the upraised sword, which had driven Lucifer and the fallen angels out of heaven and down into hell, cast a huge shadow over the boys in the late-morning sun.

The two had spotted each other in the back row of Sister Marie Rose's class. She was one of the few nuns who still taught at the Catholic school, though she dressed pretty much the same as the other women teachers. Matt Hardin had begun in kindergarten at the school, but he had never been popular. Nikolai Shakov was a new pupil and, because of this, was held suspect by his new classmates. While other students had rolled their eyes and made faces, Matt had answered the teacher's questions about the new equipment on display in the computer lab that the class had toured earlier. And Nikolai had volunteered some further information. Each had smiled at the other, recognizing someone who had more than merely a working knowledge of computers. In no time they became friends, eagerly debating the virtues of various gaming and entertainment consoles.

To the others in the class, Nikolai wasn't just an "outsider" because he was new to the school and spoke with a whisper of an accent; he was reported to have something called a "heart murmur," and the children were warned not to roughhouse with him or expect him to participate in games like baseball or soccer. Lunchroom and corner-of-the-schoolyard buzz suggested he was practically at death's door — might die any minute. This made the children shun him even more (in spite of teachers' and counselors' best efforts to set aside their fears), as if his vulnerability would somehow rub off on them.

Matt, by virtue of befriending the new boy, cemented his "loner" status. No one, it seemed, wanted to associate with either of them. Even kids sitting near them because of Sister Marie Rose's seating chart would edge away as much as they could.

The boys didn't notice or care. They were both good students who breezed through classwork and homework. They lived for the times after school or on weekends when they could get together and play computer games or simply explore the possibilities of the Internet or special applications, from site creation to photo work to, sometimes, trying to hack into protected sites—merely for the thrill of it. Computers were their lives.

"My computer helps me to live," Nikolai confided one day. "I cannot travel much or do anything very tiring. But I can go anyplace, do many things, through the screen. Who knows how far I may go? Sometimes I feel like the hero in the old Russian story my father told me over and over when I was a little boy. He was only a *muzhik*, a peasant, but he dreamed of going to heaven. He boasted, 'I will go I know not where; I will bring back I know not what.' And he got there."

"What was heaven like?"

Nikolai shrugged. "For him it was a warm house, lots of food, some gold—that part isn't so exciting. But there are many stories like that, and heaven becomes something different in each of them. What the stories really say is this: it is a mystery that can only be solved when we go there. I think it will be different for each of us." He grew very serious as he asked Matt, "What do you hope to find?"

"I don't know. Whatever Sister Marie Rose says, I guess."

"I will go there like that muzhik; I will be searching for something that I won't know until I find it. Secrets."

Usually they got together at Nikolai's house. Both his parents worked, and he was an only child. They'd bought him the most elaborate computer setup Matt had ever seen; they were convinced their son would one day have a brilliant career in computer design and programming. They also left the boys pretty much to themselves. They seemed glad that Nikolai had a friend who shared his enthusiasms and let it go at that. Mrs. Shakov was a plump, amiable woman with a mild accent; she worked in the foreign-language section of a nearby university library. Nikolai's father was an engineer who worked for a big construction firm. His accent was so thick that Matt could barely understand him.

They spent far less time at Matt's. His computer was a hand-me-down from his brother, Dave, who was a senior in high school. His sister, Melinda, two years younger, was a pest who always wanted to play computer games, even when Matt explained to her, "We aren't playing. This is important stuff." In fact, the boys were trying to construct their own computer game, which they called Far Site. Their idea was to set it on the edges of the universe, where heaven and hell lurked just beyond. In their game's plan, good and evil powers could be tapped by the two warring masters who were the focus of the game, each hoping to control everything. In fact, the boys gave themselves code names after the two masters. Nikolai was "Lightmaster" and Matt, "Darkmaster."

But Melinda would often nag their mother, who did freelance book editing at home, to "make Matt let me play, too." Driven at times to distraction by her whining, Mrs. Hardin would insist the boys include Melinda in whatever it was they were doing. Sometimes Matt would give in; more often they would simply shut off the computer and bolt for Nikolai's house where they would be undisturbed until Mrs. Shakov's return at five o'clock.

Though Saint Michael's was a Catholic school, Nikolai's family was Eastern Orthodox. But both boys had been raised in traditions that were close enough so that when they discussed matters of religion—like life after death, or what it meant to be a spirit, or what heaven or hell might really be like—they were on fairly common ground. Because of Nikolai's heart murmur, the subject of dying often came up. There were times when Nikolai became dizzy or faint at school and had to be sent to the nurse's office. Sometimes one or the other of his anxious parents would arrive to take him home from school early. Matt was shown a list of emergency numbers on the magnetic board above the telephone at the Shakovs', and he had to promise that if anything seemed seriously wrong when he was around, he would dial 911, then call both Shakov parents.

Nikolai seemed much less concerned than his parents most of the time, but sometimes, in the middle of a game of the latest version of Doom or Resident Evil (which Matt was forbidden to play at home), Nikolai's mind wandered into very different areas. One Saturday, while they were trying out different effects with Photoshop, he suddenly asked Matt, "What do you think heaven *really* looks like?"

"I don't know—angels and clouds and stuff. Like Sister Marie Rose talks about."

"I think it's another dimension, like a computer–generated world."

"Like that old movie *Tron,* where the guys go inside a computer?"

"Something like that. Maybe more like *The Ghost in the Machine,* where a guy gets electrocuted and becomes like electric energy and can move through computers and power lines."

"My folks don't let me watch scary movies," Matt confessed, feeling babyish. He wasn't comfortable with where this conversation seemed headed; he wanted to get back to working with Photoshop.

But his friend was on a roll. "I've heard scientists who say everything is just electricity. Atoms and molecules are energy. We're made up of atoms and molecules, so we're energy. And that means our souls are energy. So maybe when we die, we go someplace—like cyberspace."

"Don't let Sister Marie Rose hear you say that," said Matt, trying to make a joke of the conversation, which was getting too weird for him.

Nikolai said, "I think when we die, it's like 'delete' on e-mail. You know, the messages are gone but still occupy some sort of dimension on your computer that could be accessed. All you'd need was the right application to recover and view them again."

Matt disagreed. "You could only find an old e-mail if you didn't rewrite other information over that part of your hard drive — or didn't reformat the whole hard drive."

Nikolai grinned. "O.K., so it's not such a great example. But you get the idea."

"I guess," said Matt, unconvinced.

"It's a good idea," Nikolai insisted. "Why shouldn't we go on somewhere, be in another place after we've been 'deleted' here?"

Nikolai laughed, but Matt didn't get the joke. He tried to imagine heaven or hell, but all he could come up with for heaven was a place all sweetness and light — like one of the boring educational computer games his parents sometimes bought for him or Melinda. They were filled with cutesy characters doing nothing very exciting in settings designed to teach math or history or Spanish, which made the programs even more uninteresting. Brother and sister preferred games full of shoot 'em, blast 'em, mow 'em down action.

This made Nikolai's ideas even more difficult for Matt to grasp. Because it was easy to imagine hell as a place of slimy, slithering, roaring, snarling demons — like in Doom or something. But that only made it appealing — assuming you were sent to hell with some means of zapping any monster that crossed your path. For weaponless souls, hell really would be hellacious.

But more interesting than Adventures in Historyland.

Matt knew he was on dangerous ground here, when hell sounded better than heaven. For a moment, the thought flashed into his mind that even *thinking* such a thing might be sinful. This made him even more uncomfortable.

Again he tried to interest the other boy in a topic change, but Nikolai was in one of his "moods"—following his own line of thought so intently that Matt was forgotten. At such times, Matt just found it easier to leave. Nikolai never seemed to notice his departure. Lately the "moods" were coming more often—to Matt's increasing frustration. Today it made him angry—partly because his friend's curious ideas had made him feel uneasy. If heaven and hell weren't like he'd been taught, then, Matt reasoned, maybe nothing that his mother and father, Sister Marie Rose—all the adults in his life—believed was true. For a moment, something yawned below his familiar, everyday world—like one of those black holes out in space that could swallow up everything, even light.

He imagined the battle when St. Michael's angelic army drove Lucifer—which, he remembered Sister telling them, meant "light" or "Son of the Morning"—and the other angels-turned-devils into the depths of hell. Only now he envisioned hell as a huge black hole, swallowing the demon hordes like a shower of quickly extinguished sparks into depths from which nothing—not even light—could escape.

Hell suddenly loomed in Matt's mind not as an arena where heroes battled Doom's deadly, dangerous, zapable demons. Instead he imagined it as a lightless place of crushing weight and endless loss.

The image chilled him and gave him disturbing dreams that left him drained in the morning.

He blamed Nikolai for the anxious feeling that dogged his days and blossomed into nightmares over and over.

He no longer wanted to have anything to do with their shared Far Site concept. Too much of what the game was about reminded Matt of his new, unresolved fears.

From then on, their friendship began to fade. Nikolai talked more and more about his emerging idea that you could understand even the secrets of heaven and hell and the soul by using a computer.

He came less and less often to class. The students were told that he'd had a number of spells—something to do with his heart problems. When he did show up, he was much thinner and paler. Matt felt bad, but he kept apart. Nikolai seemed lost in some world of his own; he was totally uninterested in classwork. This was chalked up to his illness. But he raised questions, often arguing with their teacher, about what happens when someone dies. Matt sided with the majority of the class who found his former friend increasingly "creepy."

Then Nikolai didn't show up for a week.

Matt, unable to bear not knowing, e-mailed Nikolai on Thursday.

He didn't hear back until Friday.

"You are the only friend I have," Nikolai finally responded in his own e-mail, making Matt feel bad when he thought of how he had backed off. "When I try to tell things to my mother and father, they grow worried and say I am dreaming. But I see things. I've found what I call the real Far Site. I have seen ones I call the Shiny Ones. I've also seen the Terrible Ones. But when I try to show my parents, they don't see anything. Just light and dark. Now I think that only a person who believes can see. Maybe it's because I'm a child, and the Bible says you must have faith like a child. I wonder. I'm not afraid of anything I see—not even the awful things. It's all something, somewhere. I tell myself that dying might be like becoming Christopher Columbus. People said he'd sail off the edge of the world or be swallowed by dragons. But that didn't happen. He found a new world. I wish you could come with me. But I can only beg you not to forget me."

"I'll come and visit you," Matt e-mailed. But there was soccer practice and a barbecue on Saturday; on Sunday after Mass, the family spent the day visiting his aunt and uncle.

Matt didn't see Nikolai again.

On Monday, Sister Marie Rose told the class that Nikolai had passed away the day before. Everyone was upset; it was hard to imagine someone their own age gone forever. Even though no one had liked him, they felt his absence as a vaguely frightening thing. Matt had the deeply disquieting image of a single spark swallowed by vast, empty darkness—its light abruptly snuffed out.

All the fourth graders went to the funeral services later that week at St. Gregor's Russian Church.

"I'm sorry," Matt said to Nikolai's father, as everyone was leaving the church. He meant he was sorry for their loss, sorry he hadn't been a good friend to Nikolai, and sorry he hadn't visited him on the fatal weekend.

The Shakovs were so lost in their grief, they didn't seem to notice him.

So he was surprised when, four days later, Mr. Shakov

appeared at the Hardins' front door with several cartons. "Here are Nikolai's computer and files. Nikolai, he want you to have these," the man explained. Matt thanked him, but the other just shrugged and left.

When the computer was hooked up, replacing his hand-me-down, Matt immediately began calling up various applications. He felt guilty that he had gained so much because of Nikolai's tragedy—but having the elaborate computer felt wonderful.

His sister, Melinda, of course wanted to play some games, but he shooed her out of his room. He was forced to let her back when she threatened to tell their mother that his new computer was programmed with forbidden games. So he gave in and read a book on Web site construction until his sister was told to get ready for bed.

He was just getting ready to shut down the computer for the night when a message popped up: "You have one e-mail."

Sent: Saturday, September 21 2:20 PM
From: Nikolai@
To: Matt1002@universe.com
Subj: Far Site

No server, thought Matt. *Probably spam.*

But the antivirus program detected no problem. And he knew all Nikolai's applications were top-of-the-line.

The message read simply: "Nikolai here."

He hit the reply button, but all he got was a message that the source server couldn't be located.

It had to be someone playing a sick joke. He decided to play along. He began reading through the applications, coding in Far Site. At last he found what he was looking for.

It took a long time loading. The amount of memory it used was incredible; he could only imagine how much memory was built into the computer. Suddenly the screen went black, and he was afraid he'd downloaded a virus that had gotten past Nikolai's antivirus application. Then the blackness dissolved into bands of red, violet, yellow, green, and blue on a white background, rippling up and down, then side to side, like a rainbow dissolved in milk. Abruptly these patterns faded to static that was mostly white but still flecked with color. Thinking the site was jacked, Matt attempted to close it down. But nothing worked. After repeated attempts to escape, Matt decided to reset the computer, but, to his amazement, a message appeared on-screen. The colored dots arranged themselves into words against the crackling whiteness.

"Don't break contact."

Matt pulled his finger away from the reset button.

The colored flecks began to gather into a pattern. Sitting so close, he couldn't make it out. On a hunch, he stood as far back from the computer screen as he could. His guess was right: It was like one of those paintings Sister Marie Rose had shown them in class—just colored dots up close, but forming a clear picture when you were the right distance away, like pixels on a TV or computer screen.

Nikolai's face.

"That's better," said the image. The mouth moved as

words poured from the speakers that only days ago had been his. "Hello, Matt."

"This is some sort of joke, right?" Matt said.

The face took on a startled look. "No. I found my way back here. I built a kind of beacon into the computer."

Still thinking it was all some sick game, Matt asked, "Are you in heaven, then?"

"No. Maybe heaven is farther along. Most of this place is nice. But there are scary parts, too."

"All I see is white, with your face sort of painted over part of it."

"If you were here, you'd be wiped out by what you saw," answered the image Matt couldn't think of as really belonging to Nikolai.

"Yeah, well, I'll have to wait a while to find out."

But his mind was racing, trying to figure what new application Nikolai had installed that let this kind of communication take place. Not video—something very different. And who would have known about it, unless Nikolai had made a new friend in his last weeks when no one had seen much of him at school or anywhere?

"You don't have to wait," said Nikolai. "It's all electricity—energy. I can show you. Just touch the screen."

"I don't think so," said Matt sarcastically.

"You don't believe." There was such sadness, such disappointment in the voice that Matt grew uncomfortable. "It's me," the voice insisted.

"Prove it."

"You know my code name—Lightmaster. Now I'll tell you yours: Darkmaster. No one but us knows them."

Matt said warily, "Nikolai could have told someone."

"Who? You are my only friend."

"You swear?"

"Yes, I swear."

"One other thing will prove it to me," Matt said. "What did the muzhik say in that story your father told you all those years ago?"

Without hesitation, the face on the screen replied, "'I will go I know not where; I will bring back I know not what.'" Then, with barely contained excitement, Nikolai's image added, "I have done these things."

"Where are you?"

"Someplace light and dark, like I told you."

"What have you found there?"

"Secrets. How I wish I could share them with you. But you would have to be here to understand. There are no words I can use to explain."

Now Matt had to admit that he was beginning to believe. No: *believed*. The idea was terrifying and exciting all at once. He felt a dizzying rush of emotion; he was Columbus, the first man on the moon, an explorer at the edge of the universe, peering into realms beyond. And the friend he had lost forever was miraculously returned to him.

"I'm sorry for those last weeks," he said. "Not being there for you."

"You're still my friend. I wish you could be here; there is so much to see. We could explore the brightness; we could look into the dark that lies outside. I don't have the courage to get very close. But I can see strange shapes moving inside the shadows. I want to know what they are, but I don't dare by myself." Now his voice had a pleading note in it. "It wouldn't be so scary with someone else."

"Tell me about it." Matt's curiosity was growing. "Try."

"Words are no good. But I could show you a little. Just touch the screen."

Matt hesitated, sensing an overeagerness in the other. But his desire to see some part of what Nikolai was seeing—to *know* that there was something out there beyond the terrifying darkness that haunted his days, convinced him to dare.

Matt stretched out his hand, pulled it back. Then, telling himself he was a coward and a fool to distrust his friend, he pressed the palm of his hand flat against the screen. The last thing he heard, before the world flashed into white-hot sparks flecked with colors, was Nikolai saying, "I'm sorry for this trick. But we have a whole world—a whole *universe*—to discover."

For a moment, Matt was drowning in a sea of static. Then he felt Nikolai's fingers locking onto his own. He was pulled into a place of all colors and no colors, where darkness surged at the edges of a limitless expanse of blinding light. And everywhere, *everywhere,* things of light and darkness were still or moving, singing or raging, *waiting* for the boys who stood side by side.

Melinda, sneaking into Matt's room, was delighted to find her brother gone. The computer was on, but the screen was filled with static. She stared for a moment and got the impression of two small figures—one a bit more solid than the other—disappearing into a storm of rainbows and electronic snow. When she blinked, they were gone. *Just my eyes playing tricks,* she decided.

She hit reset and waited for the computer to reboot. She was glad to see that all the static had been cleared away. Happily, she settled in to play a game of Doom before Matt returned or her mother came to check on her.

field of
nightmares

None of the other kids believed Mark Jeeter's dream. But it was the heart of a long, boring summer, and building a baseball diamond in the middle of Old Man Fletcher's field didn't sound like such a bad idea. They'd have a place of their own to play in. Adults or older kids were always chasing them out of the diamond in the park. The school-yard meant playing where sliding on asphalt was a bear. The empty lot behind Tainter's Drugstore was where people were always dumping stuff so that broken glass and abandoned batteries made playing the field a real risk—especially when going deep to catch a fly ball.

Of course Mark was *weird*—there was no way around it as far as his friends were concerned. But he *had* talked Old Fletcher into letting them use his field on the outskirts of town. And he *had* gotten his uncle, who owned a lumber-yard, to agree to let them use scrap wood. Fletcher said they could scavenge lumber from the collapsed barn at the edge of the field. They'd easily be able to build a backstop and some benches.

Kazu (whose real name was Kazuyuki) Kimura reminded the others, even as they were drawing up plans for the field, "Mark is loony about this dream field." They all knew Mark watched to death his DVD of *Field of Dreams,* where some ghostly voice promises a farmer that if he builds a stadium in his cornfield, the ghosts of famous baseball players will come and he'll be able to play ball with his heroes from the past.

Mark believed he could have the same effect in Canterville. They shrugged off his ideas with, "Oh, that's just Mark," and a lot of snickering when Mark was out of earshot.

The big difference was that the guy in the movie had money to build a real stadium (even if he nearly lost his farm paying for it). And the boys only had scrap and sal-vaged wood to use. You couldn't expect any major leaguers to come back for *that,* Kazu joked. The others didn't give any thought to ghosts; they just wanted a playing field to call their own.

In point of fact, the diamond went up faster and better than anyone would have imagined because some of the boys' dads and older brothers got involved.

Of course, there wouldn't be any night games—fancy lighting was out of the question—but there were simple bleachers three rows high and an impressive backstop and even something they called their dugout but was really a clubhouse where they could hang out when they weren't playing baseball.

The day they played their first game, a scattering of families sat on the bleachers, with Old Man Fletcher and a few others drawn by curiosity or just escaping the smothering boredom that settled like a hot, dusty blanket over Canterville, Indiana, every summer.

But there was no boredom for the boys who usually managed to field two teams—sometimes fleshing out the necessary nines with a few enthusiastic sisters or good-natured older brothers. They called themselves the Canterville Cardinals and played every day.

Only Mark was disappointed. They had built the ball field, but no ghosts came—not even a minor-league spirit who'd never played in the majors. His fellow team members refused to pay attention to Mark's "spook dreams" and changed the subject when they came up.

One Saturday evening when they'd played two back-to-back games and the other team members (including Kazu's sisters, Tomoko and Haruko, who were dynamite players) had headed home, Kazu realized he'd left his backpack in the dugout. Waving to the others, he pushed open the door and found Mark sitting on one of the built-in benches along the wall. He looked up suddenly and slammed shut the book he was reading.

"Dirty pictures?" Kazu teased.

"None of your business," said Mark, shoving the book

under his folded jacket so Kazu couldn't read the title. But the book fell off the bench. Before Mark snatched it up, Kazu saw a six-pointed gold star inside a circle stamped on the black cloth cover. *Uh-oh,* thought Kazu, recognizing the symbol as having to do with devils or witches or something he'd seen in scary movies. *Well, Mark is weird,* he thought. *Maybe he's going to try to conjure up some ghostly major-league players since just building the diamond hasn't been enough.* He chuckled to himself as he left the dugout. Then, laughing out loud, he hurried across the field to catch up with his friends, while shadows lengthened across the grass.

Exactly a week later, when Kazu was sitting on his front porch, Mark came sauntering up the path. There had been no game that day — too many of the guys had gone off with their families on vacation.

"Hey," Kazu called. "What's up?"

Mark looked around and said in a voice little more than a whisper, as if he were afraid of being overheard, "Night game tonight."

They had sometimes discussed playing a game by moonlight and starlight, since the days had grown stiflingly warm. But it didn't seem quite possible.

"Too dark," said Kazu. "We've talked about it."

"It's a full moon. We're halfway there. Bring anything you can for extra light."

"When?"

"After midnight. When everyone thinks we're asleep."

"Cool," said Kazu. The idea fed into his own sense

of adventure—and he was picking up on Mark's barely contained excitement.

There were thirteen of them—not enough for two full teams, but enough for a decent practice. They had all brought extra light sources: kerosene lanterns, candles, battery-powered lamps, etc. Kazu brought two Coleman lanterns the family used when they went camping. He lit the wicks, pleased at the satisfying twin glows that resulted.

Mark's contribution was the strangest. (Except for Andy's collection of ceramic Christmas cottages with votive lights inside. "It was all I could find," he apologized.) Black candles—thirteen—"One for each of us," Mark said. "One for each of them, too."

Oh man, thought Kazu. *What time is the bus due in from Looneyville?*

"Let's play ball!" shouted Petey.

"In a minute," said Mark. While the others watched in puzzlement—except Kazu, who thought he was getting the picture and didn't like what he was seeing—Mark lit the black candles. Their flames were unwavering in the hot, still air. As soon as the last candle was lit, the nearby crickets chirruping in the grass stopped. Pulling out a pocketknife, Mark began to scratch lines in the dirt.

"Can we just, you know, *play ball?*" whined Petey, slamming his fist into his mitt.

Kazu watched with growing concern as strange letters took shape in the dust under Mark's knife blade.

"Two minutes," said Mark. Then he shouted out a string

of nonsense words that ended with, "They will come. I command it."

"I'm going home," said James. "This is too nuts — even for Mark." He stomped across the playing field, then stopped abruptly just beyond the bleachers, stretching out his hands. To the others, it looked as if he were trying to push his way through thin plastic or solidified air.

The others ran over. Their exploring hands found an invisible wall that yielded a little but would not give. Even pushing all together at one spot, they couldn't break through the barrier. Spreading out, they discovered the field was completely encircled.

"We're trapped," said James. "This is *so weird.*"

As if his words were a signal, all the boys turned to stare at Mark, who took a step away from the others.

"What have you done?" asked Kazu.

"I didn't mean this to happen," said Mark. "I only wanted them to come."

"Ghosts?"

"Yeah, I guess. Like in the movie."

"Super. Now stop whatever you've started."

"I don't know how."

"Well, I do," said James. He marched over to the circle of black candles and stomped on each one. But even when the candles were mashed flat, the unseen barrier remained.

"Now what?" Petey asked.

"We sit in the dugout," suggested Kazu. "Or we play ball. Maybe the wall will just, you know, *dissolve.* If not, our parents will figure out what to do."

"But they may not find us until morning," said Andrew.

Kazu shrugged, out of answers.

"Uh, guys, *we got company,*" said James. He pointed with his mitt toward center field. A figure was taking shape in the shadows of the clump of scrub pine that marked out of bounds, at the edge of the invisible fence.

A second figure followed, and a third—thirteen in all. They shuffled forward. They had two arms, two legs, and a head—but that was where the human similarities stopped. Each of them was about seven feet tall. Three had horns, two had tails, and several were covered with fur. Their colors ranged from dead white to blue to green to red— though one had spots, one had stripes, and one was splotches of mixed colors. There were also tusks, snouts, fangs, and a pair of bat wings that looked too small to lift the bulky creature off the ground. All these details chilled the onlookers to the bone.

Each newcomer had a black baseball cap with the same gold symbol: a six-pointed star in a circle. *Like on the cover of Mark's book,* Kazu thought. Each had a mitt—catcher's or outfielder's—and one also carried a selection of outsize baseball bats.

"They look like the monsters in *Where the Wild Things Are,*" whispered Andrew. Kazu suddenly realized that all the other boys had grouped themselves behind him, making him the point man. Mark had taken the hindmost spot.

Jimmy nudged Kazu in the back with his mitt. "Say something."

"Um, did you want something?" Kazu heard Jimmy sigh somewhere behind him. *O.K. Not a brilliant opening,* Kazu decided. But enough, as it turned out.

"Play ball," roared the head creature—the one with tusks and talons and multicolored splotches. He reminded Kazu of the action figure of Godzilla his father had brought back from his last business trip to Japan. Of course, there he was known as Gojira. For some reason, the Japanese name seemed a better fit for the thing. In the boy's mind, the monster became Gojira.

"Maybe you, um, took a wrong turn somewhere?" suggested Kazu, adding to himself, *Like you're really headed for the Monsters, Inc. play-offs.*

"Someone call us here," Gojira said stubbornly. *"Want play ball."*

"Honest guys, I didn't," whined Mark from the back.

"Oh yes, you did," said Kazu. Then he turned to the thing in front of him that was impatiently slamming his fisted, six-fingered claw into the palm of his six-fingered mitt that was made of some kind of silver-green leather thick with warts.

"This was a mistake," Mark explained, trying to sound reasonable, though his voice wavered between a whisper and a squeal. "Someone sort of called the wrong number. So you can go."

"Can't go. Path closed. Way out for us open when game over."

"Well, then, we concede," said Kazu hopefully.

"Must play. *Rules,*" insisted Gojira.

"Are there any other rules we should know about?" Kazu asked.

"Simple: you call. We come. We play. Losers eaten."

Kazu's gasp blended with collective gasps from behind him. Gojira grinned, showing a mouthful of sharp teeth framed by two up-curved tusks.

"We—uh—we couldn't, um, *eat* you guys even though we're a real good team—"

"Real good," echoed the others, but not very convincingly.

"But we're, um, *vegetarians*. We only eat vegetables," Kazu ad-libbed, pleased with the fib.

"*You* don't eat," repeated the monster. There was something odd in the way he said it that bothered Kazu. "Break rules. Not good. Your problem."

"What happens if we won't play?" said Kazu.

"You losers. Get eaten."

"*Huddle*," Kazu called. The boys formed a circle, aware of Gojira's ever-more-impatient fist slamming into his out-sized mitt.

The debate didn't last too long: to be or not to be (eaten) didn't leave them many options.

"What decide?" asked Gojira.

"Play ball," said Kazu.

One thing with several extra sets of eyes was declared umpire. When Kazu suggested this might give the monsters an unfair advantage, Gojira just looked at him unpleasantly. "No cheat. Cheater get eaten."

"Oh."

The frightened boys were somewhat relieved to find that the creatures were as clumsy as they were ugly.

One was pulled off the bag by an errant throw, allowing Andy to make it to first on a bloop single. Pop-ups often flew over the heads of creatures who seemed to take a long time to process the information—*ball coming, must catch.* And their pitching (Gojira vs. Kazu) was pathetic—high and outside, low ball, inside—

But the Canterville Cardinals weren't playing their best, either. The strangeness of the situation, plus fear of the consequences of losing, led them to make plenty of their own errors. Andy tried to steal third base and got tagged out by one of the quicker-thinking monstrosities—the red one with useless bat wings and what seemed to be a small third eye between his yellow-and-green ones. Jamie missed giveaways. Even Kazu allowed too many pitches that led to singles, doubles, and triples—though the slow-moving monstrosities couldn't always take full advantage of the opportunities. They usually swung too soon or too late, lumbered too slowly while the boys fielded balls, and managed to get knocked down—never out—by their own all-too-frequent foul balls.

The nightmarish game went into the ninth a tie: three to three. At the bottom of the ninth, there were two outs, and Kazu was up to bat. He was exhausted. He could see that all the other guys were, too. The lateness—the strain—

Gojira was pitching as crappy as ever and getting crappier.

Kazu ignored one low and inside. Then a second—so off the mark that Kazu stepped back from the plate.

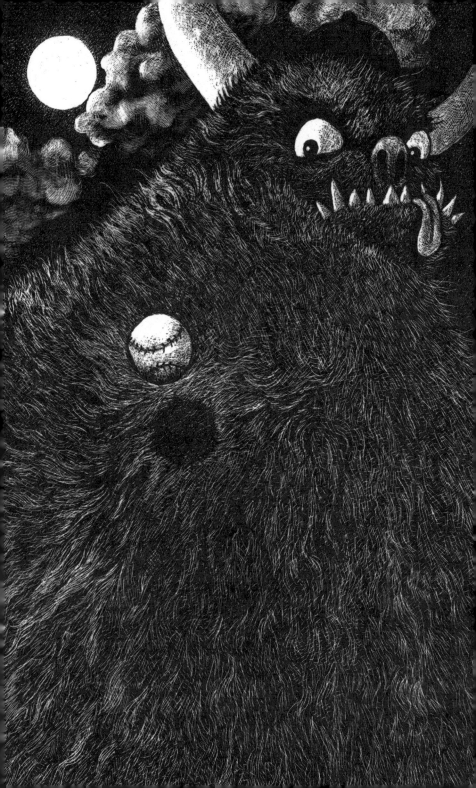

The night was cooling, but Kazu could feel sweat pouring down his face; his hands were slick on the bat, in spite of taking an extra slap of resin. He could feel all his friends' eyes on him; the pressure was incredible.

Then Gojira messed up big time. The ball came in right over the plate. Kazu was ready and swung—

Up, up and away—a long drive into center field. The polka-dot monster ran for it but managed to trip over his own tail at the last crucial moment. The ball bounced against the invisible barrier into the grass and came to rest near the polka-dot, who scrambled to untangle himself and get the ball back into play.

Kazu rounded the bases, while James, Petey, Andrew, and all his teammates chanted, "Go, go, go!"

At first base, something with a head more snake than not hissed at him.

He rounded second base; the second base beast roared at him and bared yellow fangs and jumped up and down like an angry chimpanzee. The third base thing fanned up a lizardlike crest and flicked an iguana tongue while the left fielder spewed gouts of blue lightning skyward in frustration.

The ball was hurtling back; Kazu had a chance to play safe and pause at third base, but he risked everything and slid into home, just as the blue-skinned catcher tried to tag him!

"Safe," bellowed the umpire. "Game over. Boys win. Shake hands."

They did.

"You're O.K.," said Kazu, shaking Gojira's claw, still excited by the last-minute win. Then remembering the "winner or dinner" rule, he added, "Winning is fine for us. We don't care about . . . the rest of the rules."

"Losers eaten."

"Yeah, that part. Like I said, we're vegetarians. We *can't* eat anyone, unless he's, like, a corncob or carrot."

"*You* don't eat—" said Gojira, with the exasperation of someone explaining a simple concept to a very stupid child.

"That's what I'm telling you," said Kazu, feeling equally frustrated.

"*They do —* " Gojira finished, pointing.

At the far end of the field, near the boundary trees, a fresh batch of thirteen creatures was materializing. They were (if possible) uglier than the first batch. And bigger—much, much bigger. And meaner looking. *Much meaner.* The field shook from the *thud thud thud* of their feet. Tongues—sometimes several to a single mouth—licked eagerly at the sight of the losers, standing in a miserable, resigned clump.

"Hey! No way!" cried Kazu, somehow finding the nerve to stand between the newcomers and Gojira's team.

The foremost new thing brushed him aside with an arm as thick as a tree trunk and covered with purple fur. Kazu went tumbling head over heels—stunned but not hurt. In his mind, Kazu christened this one Gyakushu or Gigantis, who battled Gojira/Godzilla in some old movies. The other boys bravely gathered around Kazu in a protective circle as he climbed shakily to his feet. They looked away as the air was filled with the sounds of tearing, chomping, chewing, gulping, and belching.

When things had quieted down again, they looked back. Nothing remained of the losers but a few bones, a tuft or two of fur, some scales, and a well-gnawed lizard crest.

"Well, that's that," said Kazu weakly. "Guess we can go."

"Go where?" Gyakushu's growl was threatening.

"Home. Away. The game's over."

"Not *one* game," said Gyakushu. "This *series.*"

The other boys looked at Kazu in shock. "What are we going to do?" whispered Andrew.

"If we don't play, we lose by forfeit," said Kazu, never taking his eyes off Gyakushu's pug-ugly face.

"And losers get eaten," said Andrew, so faintly Kazu could hardly hear him.

"So what do we *do?*" Mark whined.

"Let's play ball!" said Kazu, slapping his mitt with the best imitation of enthusiasm he could muster.

the double

It began on Anna's thirteenth birthday. She had just woken up and was lying comfortably snuggled in her blankets, anticipating her birthday lunch, when her mother and sister would take Anna and six of her best friends to eat at Soleri Gardens. She felt so grown-up. She was a teen-ager now. A young woman. As she sat up and stretched, she could almost feel some inner part of herself reaching eagerly toward adulthood. She sensed her body changing in many ways. She felt her mind grown clearer, sharper, able to see things that had been hidden before. It was like a new self was ready to be born from the body of the child she had been until this very moment.

Suddenly she heard a faint scratching at her bedroom window. Thinking it was a confused bird, she glanced toward the window beyond the foot of her bed. At first she saw only one large and several small white smudges — like the grease spots a Peeping Tom's nose and fingertips would leave on glass. Then she gave a startled gasp and blinked as the smudges solidified, and Anna was looking at a face and hand pressed against the windowpane. The features were blurry, but she could make out two large, dark eyes staring unblinkingly at her. The nails of the hand, which was clenching and unclenching, were making the *scritching* sound.

Frightened, Anna scrambled backward toward the head of her bed and pulled the bedclothes protectively up to her chin. Then she thought, *There* can't *be someone there.* Outside the second-floor window was a sheer drop to the patio below, and there was no sign of a ladder. Even as she worked this out, the image evaporated, like breath-fog on a mirror, leaving only the sun-filled glass, with a view of trees and the top of the Myersons' house behind theirs. Laughing at her fear, Anna dismissed the vision as a piece of dream that had lingered past waking.

Her favorite breakfast — French toast — was waiting. There was a gift certificate to Today's Miss boutique from her parents, a thin silver bracelet with a small silver heart attached from her older sister, Shannon, and a "Happy Birthday, Anna" spelled out in Cheerios on cardboard, framed with stiff ribbon and covered with glitter and gold paint. This was from her brother, Kevin, produced in his kindergarten class. She gave thanks and hugs all around.

The Double

It was a day made to order for a birthday celebration, Anna decided. The grass beyond the patio seemed greener; the swimming pool and sky were rich blue; the flowers massed against the back fence were crisp yellow, red, and white. But then she thought she saw a faint, gray-white shape in the shadow of the live oak, like the afterimage of a camera flash.

"What's that?" she asked.

"What's what?" asked her mother, looking at where Anna was pointing. "I don't see anything."

But her daughter was positive there was someone there—a girl. "Don't you see her? Standing by the tree. *Right there.*"

Now everybody was looking. No one else saw anything. Frustrated, Anna yanked open the glass door to the patio. But sliding the glass aside wiped the image away, like an eraser swiping a chalkboard. The garden was deserted.

Weird, Anna decided, then gave it no more thought. She lazed through the rest of the morning—showering, deciding what clothes to wear, and fiddling with her hair. But several times she caught herself peering deeper into the corner of her dressing table mirror, which reflected her window, sure that she'd caught a flicker of movement there. When she spun around for a better look, there was nothing but sunshine.

Her mother called from downstairs, "You almost ready, honey? We've got to pick up the others."

As she slipped on Shannon's bracelet, Anna stood and stared out the window. Again she had the impression that someone was standing under the oak tree, but as she stared, the illusion resolved itself into nothing more than a mix of shadow and heat-shimmer from the warming day.

When her mother called again, she hurried downstairs.

They ate outdoors under umbrellas, surrounded by ornamental tubs filled with masses of flowers. Soleri Gardens was one of Anna's favorite places to eat. She ordered her favorite dish: lemon chicken with caper sauce. Chatter punctuated with laughter bubbled around the table. Everything would have been perfect, except that Anna was increasingly convinced that she was being watched.

Without making a big deal of it, she checked out those tables she could glimpse partly or fully amid the luxuriant planter boxes designed to give privacy. Though she couldn't spot anyone looking at her, the feeling persisted. It felt like a prickling at the back of her neck and a whisper of sensation up her bare arms—like a breeze tickling the hairs.

She was so distracted, her mother asked, "Honey, are you feeling all right?"

"Just daydreaming," Anna explained, which satisfied her mother.

Soon after this, she endured, with a frozen smile, the one part of the afternoon she dreaded: the wait staff doing their hand-clapping "Hap-hap-happy Buh-buh-birthday to Anna," just ahead of the ice-cream cake her mother had preordered. Last came opening the presents her friends had brought. There was plenty of "oohing" and "aahing" as each was unwrapped, displayed, and handed round the table for closer looks.

Oddly, there were seven gift packages instead of six. The last, a small, square jeweler's box, she opened after reading the little card that wished, "Happy Birthday from your secret admirer." It was signed "A." Opening it, the girl discovered the twin of the silver bracelet her sister had given her—right down to the silver heart held in place by a single loop. She could see disappointment in her sister's eyes: Shannon had wanted her gift to be special. Now it was not.

"Who is A?" her friends asked. "A boy?" There was a great deal of giggling as her friends ran through the names of boys in her class whose names began with an A. But Adam, Alex, Alejandro, and Anthony made no connection with Anna.

"Anonymous," her mother guessed.

"Anna Nonymous," suggested Stephanie, who was the group clown. "Maybe you gave it to yourself just to make us think you've got a secret admirer."

No one knew how the package had gotten mixed in with the other presents—at least, no one would admit it, thought Anna, who was convinced one of the girls had slipped the box onto the table when no one had been paying attention. The bigger question was how A had known about the bracelet she was sure she had only mentioned to Shannon. Unwilling to let it freak her, she dropped the box and card into one of the bags holding larger gifts. Just another puzzlement in a day flecked with little mysteries.

But the sensation of being watched wouldn't go away. Even when the terrace was nearly deserted—their party lingering on—she felt compelled to scan the area, still hoping to spot a secret watcher. Now she had the added feeling that something bad was going to happen. *Where had this idea come from in the middle of celebrating?* she wondered.

"You sure you're all right, baby?" her mother asked, patting the back of Anna's hand.

"Yeah. Sure. Fine." She forced a smile. But her mother continued to shoot worried glances at her.

Anna was relieved when the party broke up. She was glad to leave the restaurant. They seemed to be the last of the lunch crowd, but Anna felt sure unseen eyes followed her.

Anna begged off dinner that night, claiming to be too full from lunch, and retreated to her room. She saw worry cloud her mother's face, but the woman said nothing.

Upstairs, Anna set the two silver bracelets side by side on her dressing table. They were identical, down to matching tiny flowers engraved on the backs of the twin hearts. She heard tapping at the window. She turned, saw nothing, and looked up into the mirror. Someone was standing right behind her, weightless hands resting lightly on her shoulders. A girl—features blurred except for eyes like twin ink smudges and long hair as dark as her own. Anna screamed, leaping to her feet as she spun around to face . . . her empty room.

Shannon tapped on her door. "Everything all right?"

"Yeah—I just pinched my finger in a drawer. I'm fine."

But she had the chilling certainty that there really had been someone standing behind her a moment before.

She crossed to the window and gazed out at the moon-splashed garden. Again she was sure that she could see a gray-white figure in the shadow of the oak tree. She was also sure that if she went to check it out, she would discover nothing but a trick of moonlight and shadow. She had to be imagining it, *had* to, she insisted to herself. Nothing else made sense. She wondered if it had to do with all the "turning thirteen" changes she was aware of in her body and her mind.

She slept with the lights on. She had disturbing dreams that she — thankfully — couldn't remember.

She stayed home Sunday, talking to a few friends on her cell phone and downloading her birthday CDs onto her iPod. She spent more time than she realized staring out the window at the yard or tuning in (between songs) to the soft Sunday house sounds, watching and listening for anything out of the ordinary. But there was nothing.

That night she burrowed deep into her blankets, eager for sleep to free her from vague worries that something unguessable might be happening to her. But sleep brought no relief. She dreamed she was running across a moonlit lawn toward a house that at first seemed strange but then slowly changed into her own home — roof and walls, door and windows reshaping themselves even as she watched. Someone was chasing her, someone with a high, sweet laugh that still managed to terrify her. She tried to call for help, but her lips felt glued shut. If only she could get to the house, she would be safe.

She ran as fast as she could, but it took forever to reach

home. At last she was close enough to see a light in one upstairs window, which she recognized as her bedroom. A girl was looking out at her, waving to Anna, silently begging her to help in some way. Behind, her pursuer laughed again; the chilling, mocking laugh frightened her beyond all reason.

At last she was close enough to the house to recognize the face in the lighted window as her own. Startled—but more afraid of what was chasing her—she signaled to the other. But her twin just smiled, shook her head, and clearly mouthed the words, "Leave me alone." Then she turned away. A moment later the light went out in the window, and the dream world went out at the same time, leaving Anna to scream silently as giggling, clutching darkness swallowed her—then released her into her bed and daylight.

She sat up, sweaty with dream fear. She could hear her mother and father moving around downstairs, fixing breakfast, talking—doing routine morning things. The sun shone cheerfully through the lacy curtains, making the flowered wallpaper and brightly patterned carpet seem even more warm and appealing.

But Anna couldn't help feeling that something was going terribly wrong in her life—that the surface brightness of things was the thinnest covering masking something shadowy and dangerous.

Later that Monday, at school, Valerie Petris said, "That was a great party Saturday. Did you buy anything at the mall on Sunday?"

"I stayed home yesterday," Anna said, feeling unreasonably uncomfortable at her friend's question.

"Then you must have a twin," said the other girl. "I thought you were just being, you know, weird, because you looked right at me when I called your name. You—I mean your look-alike—smiled at me, shook her head, then ran away. She sure looked like you, though. But I think I heard my father say everyone has a double somewhere in the world."

"Well, it *wasn't* me," Anna said so fiercely that her friend gave her a funny look, then shrugged and left to talk to someone else.

Later that afternoon, Anna was walking home and talking on her cell to another friend, Janny, who mentioned seeing Anna, again alone, going into the theater showing the latest Lindsay Lohan film. "I thought you'd seen it last week and said you *hated* it," said Janny, "so I was surprised to see you."

"It stank," said Anna shortly, "and that wasn't *me.*"

"You're sure your last name isn't Doublemint?" teased the other girl. "Because you've sure got a twin out there."

"Topic change," said Anna crossly.

"Geez! Chill!" responded Janny. "Maybe you were born twins and your mother gave the other away figuring *one* of you was all she could deal with."

"*Good-bye.*" Anna ended the call.

But having two friends make the same mistake left her feeling creepy. She already had the mysterious birthday gift of a second silver bracelet. *Duck! Here comes another mystery,* she thought sourly. She was beginning to feel like a girl detective in one of the series books she had read years before: *The Secret of the Bracelet, The Mysterious Twin.* Well, she could play detective herself, she decided. As soon as she got home, she'd ask Shannon to drive her down to Wittgenstein Jewelers. At least she could find out who "Anonymous" was, if the store kept any records.

Shannon knew Mr. Wittgenstein, the owner of the store, and explained that there had been a duplication of gifts. Anna took the matching bracelets, still in the jeweler's boxes, and set them on the counter. "Someone gave one of these to me as a surprise birthday gift," she said, "but I already had one."

The jeweler nodded gravely. "So you'd like to return one. I'm afraid I can only give store credit."

"Fine," said Anna. "But I need to know who bought the second one. I—um—lost the card and don't know who to thank."

"Your sister here bought the first one. I sold it to her myself."

"The *other* one?" Anna asked, growing impatient.

"I gather you don't know when it was purchased. Of course, if it was paid for in cash, we'd have no way of knowing. Unless . . . Kathleen!" he called into the back room. A moment later, a young woman appeared whom Anna had seen behind the counter once or twice but had never spoken to. Mr. Wittgenstein explained the situation, and Kathleen gave the sisters a curious look. "She bought it," the clerk said, pointing at Anna. "Last Saturday morning."

"No," the girl said, "I was home getting ready for my birthday lunch." She looked to Shannon, who nodded.

"Then it was someone who sure looked like you," insisted Kathleen.

"Was it paid for by charge card or check? Do we have a record?" asked the jeweler.

"Cash," said Kathleen. "I put store gift-wrap on it, and she took one of our gift enclosures to fill out later."

The sisters returned the second bracelet, using the cash receipt Shannon had kept. Anna was given a credit slip.

"Want to look for something now?" asked Shannon.

"Let's go!" was all her sister said, shoving the credit slip into her jeans pocket.

In the car, Shannon said, "That clerk was just mistaken. It was one of your friends—Deirdre or Stephanie—who looks a little like you. I'm sure she wasn't paying attention, especially if the store was busy."

But Anna wasn't so sure. These days she felt less and less sure of a lot of things.

Back in her room, she crumpled the credit slip and threw it into the wastebasket. Then she called all of her friends who had been at the party, begging them to let her in on the Anonymous joke. Each of them protested she hadn't any idea. But several were sure they had seen Anna in places she had never been, though they admitted they'd never gotten close enough to talk or to be 100 percent sure it was her.

Anna shut off her phone and lay back against the

pillows piled on her bed. Something strange was going on. But the clues didn't add up to anything. *So much for my brilliant detective work,* she thought.

On a hunch, she went to Shannon's room. Her sister had dropped her off, then gone out somewhere else. The computer they shared was kept in Shannon's room. She booted up, then began searching randomly through "look-alikes," "twins," anything she could think of. After a lot of false starts the search engine turned up "double."

Skimming through several sites, she learned that many people through the ages believed that everyone has a double, which could be a spirit or sometimes could take on a physical form. Usually one appeared in dreams. It was kind of like a person's soul, Anna decided. She continued searching. Doppelgänger, she found out, was the German name for a person's exact duplicate. The word meant "double goer." Sometimes they were seen by others in a distant location. Anna was chilled when the article concluded, "In some rare cases, individuals see their own doubles shortly before they die."

In spite of her growing worry, she searched further. A few more tries uncovered some disturbing accounts, mostly ghost stories in which the double became a real person, did away with his or her "twin," and ended up taking the original's place.

Reading this, Anna shivered, though the room was warmed by sunlight streaming through the window.

Was it possible that she was being haunted by her double? *By herself?* It seemed too crazy — yet a lot of the pieces fit, right down to the A printed on the card that had come with the second bracelet. Something that was becoming a *someone* was moving into the edges of her life. So far the other was only a shadowy figure or reflection of her, and no more than a briefly glimpsed figure to Anna's friends. But this elusive, teasing, *persistent* presence was growing stronger every day, circling closer and closer, like a shark scenting blood in the water.

The more she thought about it, the more she realized she might be in danger. But who would believe her? Her friends admitted they only *thought* they had seen her in places she hadn't been. Her sister was sure the clerk who claimed to have sold the bracelet to Anna was mistaken. She had no proof, nothing to convince anyone. When she thought about it, she found it almost as hard to convince *herself.*

She shut off the computer. For a moment she stared into the darkened screen. She saw herself reflected; then a ghostly second image appeared alongside her. It was like the double image on the TV screen when the cable was messed up.

She peered closer. She thought she could see subtle differences. The clearer reflection had the startled, frightened look she knew she was wearing. The fainter, ghostlier image was smiling, but her smile was *mean.*

"Leave me alone!" Anna croaked, her mouth and throat suddenly dry.

But the reflection only smiled more broadly. Anna was sure she heard the words, *Go away yourself,* form in her mind.

Anna squeezed her eyes shut, willing her hateful twin

away. When she opened her eyes, the darkened screen reflected only her single self. She sighed in relief, then felt her throat tighten when she heard laughter behind her. Turning, she saw herself, down to the Matches rock band T-shirt, the turquoise-and-silver Hopi belt buckle from last summer's Arizona vacation, and Shannon's silver bracelet encircling her — and the other's — left wrist.

Her double floated just outside the window. Anna screamed, "Go away!"

The other shook her head, slowly, tauntingly.

"You can't stay here," cried Anna.

Frustrated, she saw the other's mouth echo the words, *You can't stay here,* though Anna only heard the words in her head.

She remembered the stories about the doubles who became more and more real until they took over their originals' lives.

"What do you want?" cried Anna, already knowing the answer.

"I want to *be,*" replied the other. "I want to be *you.*" This time Anna was sure she heard a real voice — not merely a whisper in her head.

"You can't be me," said Anna, her own voice hardly more than a whisper.

"I'm already a piece of you," her image said. "A little part that isn't satisfied to be less than the whole of you. All those wonderful feelings — those birthday feelings — woke me up. There's no going back." She stretched out a hand, pressed it against the window. "Take my hand. Reach into the window" — suddenly the voice was behind Anna. She spun around and saw the second Anna afloat in the mirror, the flat of her hand pressed against the inside of the glass. "Or reach into the mirror. *Let me free. I won't be shut out any longer. I won't.*"

Now she was outside the window again. *"Go away!"* screamed Anna to the window image.

Frantic, she picked up a heavy crystal paperweight Shannon kept beside the computer and hurled it at her tormentor. Too late, Anna thought: *She can't really cross into my world. She can't be anything more than a reflection to me — something that's only real when I'm not around. She'll always be outside the window or inside the mirror.*

Then the window exploded outward in a shower of sparkling glass fragments. All barriers were down. Anna had the stomach-churning double vision of an airplane window shattering, sucking the air, the life, out of an airplane into the night beyond — or a submarine hull breached, letting frigid dark water in. Her real self — a bundle of thoughts, memories, dreams — her soul — poured into the outerness; she was aware of her other self rushing past to flood her suddenly emptied body. An instant later, Anna felt her true self shattering into bits and pieces that followed the smashed window into the sunshine and rained down onto the lawn below.

Anna's mother and Shannon arrived in Shannon's bedroom at the same time, drawn by the crash of breaking glass. Anxiously they searched the empty room. Asking each other the same questions that neither could answer, they approached the now-vacant window frame carefully, surprised to find no glass on the rug and none on the window ledge. The glass seemed to have been drawn out by some huge vacuum cleaner and emptied into the yard below. The lawn sparkled with glass particles glittering like heavy morning dew.

Someone was standing at the far edge of the lawn, beyond the shattered glass in the shadow of the oak. Anna's mother had to shade her eyes against the sun's glare to make out the figure. "Anna, is that you?" she called.

"Yes," the girl answered.

"Are you all right? What happened?"

"Fine. I don't know. The window just sort of *exploded*. It was *so weird*."

"You aren't cut, are you?"

"Nope. I was back here when it happened."

"The glass must have been defective or something," Anna's mother said. "Maybe your father can figure out what happened."

Shannon said, "Glass doesn't blow up or out or whatever."

"I'm sure I read somewhere that it can happen. Maybe the sun's heat . . . Well, it doesn't matter since no one was hurt."

"What's she holding?" asked Shannon, pointing to her sister, who clutched what seemed to be a sphere of sun-bright glass.

"We'll find out in a minute," her mother said. Then she leaned through the empty window frame and called to her younger daughter, "Are you coming in?"

"Yes," the girl shouted back. "I've been outside long enough. I'm ready to come in."

Brushing the last strands of grass from the paperweight that had landed safely on the lawn, trailing glass like a comet followed by its tail, the girl carefully stepped around the window fragments in which countless tiny images of herself beat their fists against countless glass-sliver prison walls and screamed soundlessly.

johN moulDy

It was on the third day after they moved in that Billy Bergfeld's father suddenly came upstairs from working in the basement of their new home and began rummaging through cartons of as-yet-unpacked books. With a grunt of satisfaction, he pulled out an old book of Walter de la Mare's poetry, opened to the page he wanted, and recited:

> *"I spied John Mouldy in his cellar,*
> *Deep down twenty steps of stone;*
> *In the dusk he sat a-smiling,*
> *Smiling there alone."*

Billy wondered what had made his father suddenly think of the poem. The boy hadn't heard those lines for ages. Billy hated the poem because it had made him afraid to go into the basement of their old house. His dad loved the works of Walter de la Mare and insisted on reading the verses to his son when Billy was a baby in his crib. But for the child, the rhyme was the stuff of nightmares.

Now old fears came back. In the days that followed, Billy imagined John Mouldy moving through the new house at night after taking shape in a corner of the cellar where mingled moonlight and streetlight seeped through the dusty window and illuminated the patch of gray-green mold that his father was trying to get rid of. Ray Bergfeld scraped, bleached, and sanded the wall, but the fungus always came back. On the few occasions when he was forced to go downstairs to run an errand, Billy tried to avoid looking at the moldy wall. But he couldn't. And every time it seemed to take a different shape—a leering face, a prancing goblin, a misshapen figure reaching out for him. All were aspects of the same thing in his mind: John Mouldy. Each visit was agony for the boy whose imagination worked overtime.

John Mouldy stalked his dreams, too—a blurry figure rising out of gray shadows, ripping free of fungus-coated walls, and endlessly pursuing and almost overtaking the boy—until Billy woke up, just before fuzzy, gray fingers closed over his shoulder.

His father's never-ending battle with the mold was an endless topic of discussion at the breakfast and dinner table.

"Maybe we should have it tested," Billy's mother, Anita, suggested. "Maybe it's one of those dangerous molds.

Remember what happened at the college last year? They built that new dorm, but they didn't paint properly or seal the walls or whatever, and now they're going to have to tear it down because it's filled with toxic mold."

"Let me think about it," said his father, and Billy knew that meant "no." He'd heard the same words every time he'd asked for things—Rollerblades, computer games, a new bicycle—none of which appeared.

Time after time the mold got sprayed out, scraped off, scrubbed away—and it always came back. The stuff frightened Billy and his mother—though for different reasons. His father viewed it as an irritation and a challenge. Billy didn't dare voice his fear that the stuff was somehow sinister—like the lurking, threatening, gray-green figure that haunted his daydreams and nightmares. His father would have no patience with such "garbage." He ignored his wife's reasonable fears. Billy knew the man would utterly reject and belittle his son's linking the lines of an old poem with what was, to his father, nothing more than the result of dampness, flawed construction, and age.

Their "new" house was a vintage house in the oldest section of Arkham, Massachusetts. His parents were planning to turn it into a bed-and-breakfast. And Ray Bergfeld insisted on doing all the work himself—or most of it. Sometimes he called in Mr. Costaine and his son, Lance. People made fun of Lance—"not the sharpest knife in the drawer," Billy's father commented more than once—but Billy liked him. Lance was big and friendly and let the boy paint or hammer or do a few things when Ray wasn't around to say, "Stay out of the way, Billy. They've got work to do, and I'm paying them by the hour." In Lance's company, Billy wasn't afraid to go down to the basement.

Today Lance was putting up metal shelving for storage against the wall underneath the window. The late-afternoon sun was slanting in the window. It highlighted the gray-green patch of mold that continued to resist his father's every attempt at eradicating it. Now the mold patch looked almost like an old man, hands folded, smiling (not a pleasant smile), watching them.

Billy, sitting on the floor nearby, avoided looking at the fuzzy near-image, focusing instead on screwing together nuts and bolts under Lance's direction.

Suddenly Lance gave a small, startled cry and said, "That moved."

Billy looked up to see his friend pointing at the opposite wall. Caught in a rectangle of fading sunlight from the window, the moldy figure took on a silvery sheen. A trick of the light made it look almost man-sized now. "You're imagining things," said Billy uneasily. "It's just a patch of mold."

"It slid. To the side. Like a crab or a spider," Lance said stubbornly.

"I'm finished with another shelf," Billy said, trying to draw Lance's attention back to the job at hand. But Lance was absorbed by the scuzzy patch on the painted brick wall. He reached toward it —

"Don't," warned Billy, scrambling to his feet and grabbing Lance's elbow. "My mother says it might be poisonous."

Lance wasn't listening. He shrugged off Billy's hand. The big man-boy stretched his hand out. His fingertips brushed the thick patch of mold and gently slid down the wall.

"So soft," he murmured.

"You shouldn't—" Billy persisted.

But the other refused to listen. First he raised his fingertips to his nose, inhaled, and sighed happily. Then he touched his fingers, still dusted with gray-green fuzz, to his lips, sucked on them a moment, then smiled.

"So sweet," he murmured.

"This is not good," Billy muttered to himself. His friend took two more tastes of the mold before Billy's dad tromped down the stairs.

"Aren't you done yet?" he demanded, glaring at Lance, who continued to stare in a kind of wonderment at the bearded wall. "I'm paying you by the hour here!"

Lance blinked rapidly several times, like a man waking from deep sleep, or someone snapping out of a trance at the clap of a hypnotist's hands. Had tasting the mold affected him like some kind of drug? Or maybe the mold gave off a scent that only Lance could smell—like flowers that drew insects into the deadly embrace of a pitcher plant or Venus's flytrap. Hadn't Billy heard somewhere that the spores from mold could mess with a person's mind? Mold could be halluci-*something*—anyway, make you see things that weren't there. Or maybe things that really were there but that no one else could see. Maybe it was dangerous, like his mother said—but the poison affected different people in different ways. Made his father suddenly think of an old poem. Gave Billy nightmares. And made Lance . . . want to touch and even *taste* it. Maybe Lance reacted this way because he was different: his brain worked differently. But why would the mold try to attract a person?

"Sorry, Mr. Bergfeld," Lance said, clearly back to reality.

"And what are you doing?" Ray asked his son.

"Helping," said Billy, half angry at being treated like a baby, half fearful of what Lance had done.

"Well, Lance can finish on his own. You go upstairs and help your mother."

Billy shot Lance one last look. The guy had returned to the shelving, but as the boy followed his dad upstairs, he watched over his shoulder. He saw the younger man glance across at the patch of mold and give a secret smile. In the fading sunlight, the boy could have sworn he saw an answering smile form in the moldy "face."

The family ate early, because they were having company after dinner.

Arnold Moore was a professor of history at Miskatonic University, on the outskirts of Arkham. His wife taught science at one of the high schools. To Billy, it seemed that the guy talked way too much, and Mrs. Moore said almost nothing, which made them equally tiresome. But they were old family friends—Dr. Moore and Billy's father had gone to college together. It was Dr. Moore who had suggested the Bergfelds move to Arkham when Ray let it be known that he wanted to leave the business world to become an innkeeper.

Billy thought the move a big-time mistake—partly for the friends and school he had to leave behind, but mostly for the creepiness of the house, from its shadowy attic to the moldy basement.

"I thought I'd prepare a history of this place as a house-warming gift," the professor said with a nervous laugh that was more like a cluck. "But it wasn't, er . . . quite what I expected."

"In what way?" asked Billy's dad, sounding not terribly interested.

"Well, er . . . little pitchers have big ears," he said and indicated Billy with a sideways nod of his head.

Taking the hint, Billy's mother said to him, "Why don't you go watch TV?"

Billy excused himself and went into the adjoining family room, gently closing the door behind him. He turned on a cartoon show but crept back, pushing the door open just a crack.

In the other room, satisfied that the boy was out of earshot, Arnold Moore continued, "Back when this place was built, it was one of the most popular inns on the Arkham Post Road. The owner, Rupert Beene, saw that it had all the most modern conveniences for the time. But from the get-go it had an . . . er, oh . . . *unsavory* reputation. There was talk that some travelers—usually single men—drummers—"

"Musicians?"

"No—that's an old name for traveling salesmen—checked in but never checked out."

"What did they call it? The Roach Motel?" Billy's dad said, breaking into a loud laugh at his own humor.

Billy stifled a chuckle at the bad joke.

"Anyhow," Dr. Moore went on, clearly annoyed at the interruption, "people got suspicious. A group of angry citizens set out one night to search the house and discover the truth of the accusations. The men ransacked the house. In the basement they found human bones — lots of them — buried in lime, just under the floor. The authorities took them away and identified some victims. All of them had been one-time guests at the inn."

"What happened to Mr. Beene?" Billy's mom asked.

"The . . . um . . . *official* story is that he had somehow gotten wind of what the men were planning. Supposedly he fled into the night just ahead of the vigilantes. Rumor had it, he took a lot of his ill-gotten gains with him."

"You don't believe that, do you, Arnie?" Ray Bergfeld asked.

Another cluck of a laugh. "Oh, it has nothing to do with what I believe. But there is . . . er . . . a second set of rumors that say the men surprised Beene, found the evidence of what he'd been doing, and carried out a kind of what you might call 'rough justice.'"

"Meaning . . . ?" Billy's mom asked.

"Arnold," said Mrs. Moore warningly — the first thing she'd said in an hour, by Billy's estimate.

Unwilling to cut off his story in midtelling — especially not with an audience fully drawn in — Dr. Moore concluded, "They reportedly beat him senseless, then sealed him, unconscious, bound and gagged, but alive, in a wall. They went away and left him to a slow, horrible death."

Billy, who hated closed, cramped places, could all too

vividly imagine what it would be like sealed without room to move, tied up, gagged, unable to call for help or make a sound, growing weaker from lack of air and food and water. True, the man had been a murderer, had committed terrible crimes, but such a death seemed beyond justice to Billy. And how much worse the suffering if Beene could hear voices from beyond the wall—how he must, in his last minutes, have grown to hate anyone who was able to live and move freely and escape into the open sunshine while he descended into an agony of hunger and thirst, suffocation and darkness. In the end, Billy imagined, there would be only pain and hatred. Even the pain might fade as consciousness ebbed away. But the hatred—that might linger. Billy remembered watching a TV show about ghosts where someone said hauntings were a dying person's emotions, feelings so strong they remained recorded on things and places, like music on a CD. Billy imagined a dying man's hatred no longer attached to a living person, but pure hatred existing as a force, directed at anyone who came under its influence. . . .

Hatred growing like mold, surviving beyond death.

The boy left off his horribly vivid imaginings when he heard his father ask, "And the money? If Beene didn't take it, what happened to it?"

"The men claimed they found no trace. Still, all of them seemed to live a little better after that. Not like princes, perhaps, but certainly not like paupers, either. When the place was taken over by new owners, the first stories began to surface that it was haunted. Only no one reported exactly what the haunting involved. People saw—"

"—imagined—" interrupted Billy's father.

"—lots of different things. But the majority of . . . um, *disturbances* seem to have involved the basement."

"Where the bodies of the victims were found," finished Ray Bergfeld. "Sounds like a pretty typical ghost story."

"Have you seen anything out of the ordinary since you've been here?" the other man asked.

Ray laughed. "Not a spook. Nothing unusual, except that the east wall of the basement stays moldy, but it's just the damp. That wall backs against the hillside. It's always wet, so you get mold." His bored tone of voice made it clear that he wanted a topic change.

Mrs. Bergfeld offered dessert and coffee, and the subject switched to a local election. Billy tried to watch TV, but he couldn't keep his attention on the show. He kept thinking: What if the wall where the mold grows is where they sealed up Mr. Beene? Maybe the mold is some part of his hatred that lingered after he died and is now seeping through the wall, getting into the light, getting into people's minds.

He thought of telling his father—but quickly reminded himself that his father had no patience with his son's "overactive imagination." And if he broke open the wall himself and there was nothing behind it—no skeleton or mummified corpse of Mr. Beene—then his father would ground him forever. And if there *was* something there, who knew what he might unleash on his family or the town? Unable to arrive at any real answer, he finally let himself get caught up in the cartoon world of *Zelda the Zombie.*

Much later that night, Billy awoke suddenly — grateful to have escaped another John Mouldy nightmare. But his feeling of relief didn't last. His room, in the middle of being refurbished, seemed alive with whispers. Faint voices seemed to be muttering from behind the sheets of plastic gently rippling over gaps where the plaster was ripped out or in folds of canvas softly flapping in front of the windows.

He was fully alert now, listening. The house was a house of whispers. Soft. Fuzzy. Hinting everything, telling nothing. The more intently he listened, the surer he was that there was something murmuring that could not be explained away as fluttering plastic or canvas. Now he was certain it was coming from the hall outside his partly opened door.

"Mom. Dad," he called, softly at first. Getting no response, he called more loudly. When there was still no response, he climbed out of bed, pulled on his bathrobe and slippers, and hurried down the hall. He knocked, then pushed open their bedroom door.

The whispering persisted, though here plastic hung limply, and canvas dangled from scaffolding in the empty room that seemed curiously stuffy and airless, though the breeze outside had the trees swaying and bobbing.

"Mom. Dad," he shouted. Only faint whispers rising from the stairwell answered him. He ran along the upstairs hall, knocking on, then pushing open, every door. Nothing. Growing more and more worried, he hurried down the stairs, then dashed through empty room after empty room — living room with furniture draped in more plastic, dinner table still cluttered with dishes from the after-dinner party, kitchen with pots soaking in the sink —

The door to the basement hung open.

Floating up from the darkness below came a susurration of sounds: mutters, breathing, padding footsteps, something solid shifting slightly, as though bumped.

"Mom? Dad?" His own voice was barely above a whisper now.

But from downstairs came an answer, "Here. Here. Here."

Maybe it was his mother, maybe his father. It was like both their voices — but not quite. But it was *enough* in the huge, empty, sighing, whispering house to know *someone* was there.

He started to descend the stairs, then paused three steps down when he heard what sounded like a giggle, half-smothered by an unseen hand. He had the impression of a child, barely able to contain his excitement, planning to scare an unsuspecting newcomer.

"Who's there?" he called into the darkness.

"Mom. Dad," came the whispers.

"Mom. Dad," he repeated. Fearful. Hoping.

He continued warily down the stairs, still uncertain, still on guard.

The cellar was empty. But different. "Mom. Dad," he called into the dank shadows that clung like dark mold to

the walls and piled up like black snowdrifts in every nook and corner.

"They're here," answered a voice, much clearer and louder than before.

Billy froze on the last step, staring at the opposite wall. The full moon had replaced the sun, shining a pale rectangle on the wall. But the patch of mold was changed. Afraid to step off the bottom stair, Billy peered closer. It was darker, bigger, and more misshapen than ever.

"Mommy. Daddy," he said, his voice not much more than a croak.

"There, there," said the figure, fuzzed with gray-green mold that looked like, but couldn't possibly be, Lance. It was pulling away from the wall now. With one hand it pointed at the two shadow-draped, still figures sprawled at its feet. The wind burst open the outer door to the cellar. Moonlight flooded in, revealing the smears of gray on the faces, throats, and robes of Ray and Anita Bergfeld. They both wore expressions of shock and terror.

Billy gave a moan, spun, and flung himself up the stairs.

Footsteps pounded up the steps behind him. He knew Lance could never run that fast, as uncoordinated as he was. But, he realized, it was no longer Lance who was after him. It was his nightmare, and he knew he could never outrun his nightmare in the real world any more than he could in his sleep. And this time there was no escape into wakefulness.

There was a brief scuffle. Some shouts. Then the *bump-bump-bump* of something hauled carelessly down wooden steps. Then a silence fell over the house, broken only by the soft *thump* of a book falling off a shelf in the living room. It landed open to the page on which an observer — if there had been more than shadows present — could read:

> *"I spied John Mouldy in his cellar,*
> *Deep down twenty steps of stone;*
> *In the dusk he sat a-smiling,*
> *Smiling there alone."*

green thumb

When school was in session, Lateesha could only visit her garden late in the afternoon, after the municipal bus left her off in front of the projects, where she lived with her mother and aunt. Now, in summer, she went early in the morning, while it was still cool, before the sun began to heat up the little spit of land jutting into San Francisco Bay. By eleven, the family apartment in the complex would begin to warm up—especially since it faced east toward Berkeley and Oakland and into the rising sun. Then the air—barely disturbed by the clattery old fan—would grow stifling in the heat.

Greenpoint was the wrong name for the little peninsula. By June all the wild grasses in empty lots and untended garden plots had dried to yellow-brown. Here and there, scattered trees and hardy bushes struggled to survive the heat and neglect.

Because there was no water supply near her garden, the girl carefully filled four big plastic jugs from the faucet at one corner of the three-story apartment building she lived in. These she tied two and two at either end of a piece of clothesline rope. When she was ready, she positioned the rope behind her neck and over her shoulders. Then, looking like a Chinese laborer from her history book, she made her way to the empty lot behind what was left of the Thurgood Marshall Memorial Playground—a sagging rectangle of cyclone fencing enclosing a sad collection of rusting metal swings and slides and dried weeds. Hardly anyone went there, except for the older boys who played basketball on the cracked court, dreamed hoop dreams, and ran off any younger kids who dared approach their turf.

Lateesha skirted the western extension of the fence. The place was deserted this early. The field behind the basketball court was an expanse of crinkly brown grass, knee-high, that swept up to a cluster of abandoned cars, a stove, a doorless refrigerator—castoffs from the tenements that made up Greenpoint, perhaps the most ignored part of San Francisco.

Some distance beyond the junk wall was a half circle of tall Scotch broom bushes. Their dusty, dark green leaves, small yellow flowers, and seedcases like tiny gray pea pods helped screen her garden from prying eyes.

Mainly she wanted to avoid Tyson Moore. Tyson had it in for her, though she had never given him a reason to dislike her. But he was mean whenever he got the chance. Her mother had assured her, "That boy's just jealous of you because you're smarter and you're going places." Sometimes she wondered if he was jealous of the fact that she had a loving mama and aunt, because Ty had only an indifferent mama and a father and two older brothers who were always beating on him. Maybe it was just the way the world worked; in the projects, too many people would pull you down a lot faster than they'd offer a hand up.

It was hard work carrying the water jugs so far. But when she'd tried to make a garden nearer the apartment building, kids playing tag or ball would run through it. Or Tyson and his friends would tear it up. So Lateesha had found this hidden place. Children rarely played in the field where rusty metal and broken glass and stinging nettles and blackberry thorns made it a hazard. Adults only came to leave more trash.

There was another reason folks avoided the field—an old house with most of the paint worn off that kids called "the witchy house." They whispered to one another that the old woman who owned it was a witch from New Orleans who had voodoo powers. There were rumors of strange lights and cries in the night and even people—mostly children—who had disappeared when these lights were seen and cries were heard.

Lateesha didn't believe the stories. But she was curious about the person who lived there. The backyard of the house was separated from the field by a hedge taller than a man. The house fronted a dead-end street called Comstock

Court. It was one of a row of old homes—barely more than shacks—that had been built long before the projects had gone in. Most of the others had been torn down or had fallen down. But a few people still lived there.

The girl imagined a beautiful garden on the other side of the hedge. She could see the tops of hollyhocks and sunflowers and a little tree whose leaves were plum-colored. Once she had gone up to the hedge and found a spot where she could just squeeze through. But her nerve gave out when she heard someone singing a spiritual that she knew from church. Still, she had pushed far enough in to glimpse masses of red, blue, yellow, and white blossoms, which were rivaled by the purple-and-pink blossoms printed on the muumuu worn by the stout old woman who tended the flowers. To Lateesha, it almost seemed as though she were singing *to* the plants. She couldn't see what the woman looked like because her back was to the girl and she wore a big round straw hat that hid her head and face. Afterward, once or twice, the girl had strolled by the front of the cottage, which was covered with passionflower vines and honeysuckle, while rows of rosebushes divided the sidewalk from the porch. But she had never glimpsed the gardener's face.

Lateesha reached her own garden in the shelter of the broom bushes. She had some geraniums and daisies and a small tea rosebush. She also didn't mind a few of the prettier growing things that others might have dismissed as weeds: goldenrod, aster, milkweed—she even had a lone sunflower beginning to sprout. She was learning what things would survive here. She had purchased some of the seeds and seedlings on the rare occasions when she could get to the grocery store fifteen blocks away; it had a small gardening-supplies section. But these had simply withered away or refused to sprout. Some of her survivors came from cuttings she had begged from neighbors who grew a few things indoors or in window boxes, safe from playing or marauding kids.

She worked happily for an hour and had just gotten to her last duty — carefully portioning out the water from her plastic jugs to the thirsty plants. She was wetting the roots of the yellow-and-white daisies that (she imagined) were eagerly awaiting their morning drink when a shadow fell across her arms.

She looked up to see Tyson Moore standing between her and the sun. "She grow *weeds*," he said to the three boys who were hanging back a little. "She *crazy*," he said with a grin. The others grinned back.

Lateesha slowly got to her feet, holding the rope that was tied to the three empty water jugs and the full fourth. She turned to Ty and asked, "What do you want?"

For a moment, his smile slipped in the face of her challenge. Then his eyes flicked to his backups, assuring him that they were still there. Facing the girl, who was outnumbered four to one, he said, "Nothin' much. Just wanted to see what you was up to, sneakin' out here mos' mornin's." He made a show of studying the plants. "Got some pretty things here. Might take some home to my mama." He reached down and tore up a fistful of daisies.

Lateesha, saying nothing, tightened her grip on the rope, keeping her eyes locked on his.

Ty raised the flowers to his nose, made a face, then cried, "They stink. Can't give these to my mama." He flung the daisies every which way. "Nothin' here worth crap! Just weeds, weeds, weeds!" Every time he shouted the word, his Converse-clad foot trampled a plant. In a minute, the daisies were crushed. "Got to get rid of these weeds," he said. One of the other boys had begun kicking and tromping on her geraniums.

"Stop!" Lateesha yelled. Then, hardly aware of what she was doing, she grabbed the rope, hefted the filled water jug, and swung it so that the full weight of it slammed Ty in the back. The blow knocked the wind out of him. With a *whumpf!* he went sprawling at the base of a cluster of broom. He lay still. The other boys just stared stupidly at their fallen leader.

"You killed him, girl," said one. Lateesha, just as shocked, remembered his name was Jerome.

No one moved until Ty moved. Shaking his head, he rose to his hands and knees.

Relief (that he wasn't dead) and fear (what would he do to her now?) kept her uncertain and unmoving. She held defensively to the rope.

Jerome and one of the other boys hauled Ty to his feet. Ty was still trying to catch his breath, trying to talk. She couldn't make out much of what he was saying, but she heard him gasp, "Go-gon-gonna get you good, you b—"

Before he finished, Lateesha dropped the rope and ran.

They were after her in a minute, with Tyson, still not fully recovered, loping behind the other three.

She ran toward Comstock Court, hoping that, without the hazards of the field, she could outrun them on the road or find an adult to help her.

But the boys were smart enough to outflank her. Ty and Jerome began circling left; the other two curved right. The girl guessed they were going to trap her against the hedge-row behind the witch's house.

And they were succeeding; they reached the ends of the hedge before she had a chance to scramble over the crumbling stone wall behind one deserted house or escape down the alley that separated the witch's house from the house next-door. Though someone lived here, drawn yellowing blinds on every window made it clear that the inhabitant wanted nothing to do with the world outside.

Her only hope of escape was through the hedge at the spot where she had pushed through before. The boys were closing in from both sides when she plunged into the weak place in the green barrier. To her surprise, it seemed easier going than she remembered—almost as if the greenery were giving her safe passage. Behind her, she could hear Ty and the others grunting as they followed her, but the hedge seemed to be giving them far more trouble than her.

She stumbled into the yard beyond. Her foot caught on a stone, and she sprawled on the soft green lawn in front of what seemed a curtain of gold-and-orange blossoms, but she quickly realized it was the pattern on the muumuu worn by the mysterious gardener. Uncertainly, Lateesha looked up into a broad face, largely shaded by the straw sun hat she had seen before.

"Well, look at the hedgehog come to visit," said the woman. She reached down a large brown hand and helped Lateesha stand.

"They're chasing me—" the girl began. Then Ty popped out of the brush, with Jerome right behind. She could hear the other two boys battling their way through the hedge, just behind Jerome.

With a quick movement, the woman pushed Lateesha behind her. Then she drew in her breath, placed her hands on her hips, and—crazy as it seemed—appeared to grow half again as tall as she had been a moment before.

"What do you think you're doing?" she demanded. Ty and Jerome blinked in astonishment at her booming voice. "You're *trespassing*," she answered her own question. "I'll have the police all over your behinds if you don't turn right around and get back the way you came."

Tyson began to bluster, but Jerome whispered frantically in his ear. Lateesha caught only the words, "She *witchy*, man," but she could guess what was going on.

Clearly the woman had heard, too. She held her two big hands out in front of her, palms up. "I got plenty of power to fix the likes of you," she said.

Ty drew himself up to meet the challenge. Jerome decided to play it cooler and retreated back toward the hedge. There was some whispering between him and the two boys who had held back in the prickly shelter of the greenery. Then Jerome and the others were gone.

Ty stood his ground and glared at the old woman. But Lateesha, watching from behind her protector, could see his resolve weakening without the other boys to support him.

The woman shook her head, saying, "Hate to do this, boy, but you're bringing it on yourself." She reached into the pocket of her muumuu and took out a handful of what looked to Lateesha like plain old dirt. "This here's goofer dust—dirt fresh off a grave. Know what it does?"

Ty shook his head, eyes glued to the handful of soil.

"Well, you're about to find out," said the woman. She muttered a couple of strange words as she opened her palm, then blew on the dirt so that it erupted in a cloud.

Ty was gone before a speck of the dust touched him. Lateesha heard him crashing and cursing his way back through the hedge.

She asked, "What does goofer dust do?"

"Heck if I know, honey. That was just plain old dirt. Can't work in the yard and not get a little dirt in your pockets and shoes. Come inside, and I'll fix you some iced tea—green tea, that's the best—and I've got some ginger-snaps, too."

Everything in the little house was old and worn, much of it—curtains, tablecloth, napkins—patched and repatched. But it was all clean and neat. They sat in the kitchen while Lateesha explained what had happened.

At last the gardener, Bernice, said, "You love growing things, don't you?"

"Yes, ma'am."

"Here, let me look at your hands."

Lateesha dutifully presented her hands to the woman. Peering through a pair of the thickest glasses the girl had ever seen, the woman turned her hands over, studying them front and back. Finally she sat back and said, "You got a green thumb, yes indeed."

Lateesha looked at her thumbs. "Is that bad? Do I need medicine?"

Bernice laughed. "It's a *gift!* You got a feel for growing things. You just need a real garden to let it happen."

The girl sighed. "Ty and the others have smashed my garden for sure."

"Don't worry about that. You can come and work in my garden. I'm getting on; I need help. You're the answer to my prayers."

After their talk, Bernice walked Lateesha home so she could meet the girl's mother and aunt. But before they left the old woman's house, she pulled a necklace with a silver chain out of a desk drawer. Instead of a jewel, the chain held a tiny, yellowish seed embedded in a drop of clear plastic with a silver circle around it.

"Anyone says anything to you," said Bernice, "you just show them this and say the witchy woman gave it to you. Tell them I will *know* if anyone troubles you. But they won't," she assured the girl with a shake of her head.

Lateesha held the plastic bead up to the light and studied the seed.

"It's a mustard seed," Bernice said softly. "Bible tells us faith is like a mustard seed. It's the smallest seed of all, but when it grows, it springs up just like a tree so even birds will nest in it. You keep that little seed of faith in yourself, and in what the future holds, and there's no telling what it will grow into."

Wearing the necklace worked, just as Bernice said it would. Word got around Greenpoint that the girl was under her protection. Not everyone believed the old woman had a power, but no one wanted to find out for sure.

Every morning Lateesha went to the cottage on Comstock Court. Side by side, she and Bernice would plant and water and weed and mulch the front and back and sides of the place—all of which were gardens. One of the side gardens was a vegetable garden, and the girl often took a bagful of tomatoes or cucumbers or lettuce home with her, to the delight of her mother and aunt.

One afternoon, just before the school year began, Bernice stood on the lowest back porch step, hands on hips, nodded, and said, "You *sure* got the green thumb. My garden never looked so good."

Lateesha didn't say anything, just stood on the lawn feeling pleased enough to burst.

When classes started again, each afternoon she would get off the bus two stops early and help Bernice until she had to go home for dinner.

At school, she was aware of Ty and Jerome and some of the other kids always watching her. Then they made a big show of ignoring her in the cafeteria or at recess or on the bus. She always wore her silver necklace with the mustard seed and she was never afraid. It was like Bernice was at her side—a guardian angel in a flowered muumuu and straw hat.

One day, Ty stopped her in the hall at school, just before the first bell. She tried to walk around him, but he kept stepping in front of her, blocking her way. The only other kids in the hall were his friends or were afraid of the bully; she knew they wouldn't help her. He suddenly reached out and hooked the silver necklace chain with his finger. "That some pretty fancy bling you wearing."

She tried to disentangle the thin chain, but he kept it firmly twined around his finger.

"You got this from that ol' witchy woman."

Lateesha nodded.

"She got a lotta this stuff?"

The girl shrugged. She had the uncomfortable feeling that Ty's greed was pushing aside any fear that lingered after his encounter with the witchy woman. Suddenly afraid of what she was seeing in Ty's eyes, Lateesha shook her head. "She hasn't got anything you want. Leave us both alone." She tried to pull back. But he gave her necklace a tug; Lateesha was afraid he would snap it away. Fortunately the appearance of a teacher forced Ty to let go of the chain. The girl hurried down the hall to her first class as the bell sounded. But she was aware of Ty's eyes following her.

She made a point of avoiding him in the days that followed. And she wore the necklace under her blouse.

The following Saturday morning, Lateesha ran around the corner onto Comstock and stopped, puzzled, then fearful. Several police cars were parked in front of Bernice's house. Yellow security tape covered the front of the house. When the girl tried to find out what had happened, she was told to go home by a police officer, who wouldn't let her near the cottage. Spotting the neighbor lady who had sometimes visited Bernice, bringing gifts of cookies or a pie and leaving with bouquets of flowers, she asked what had happened.

The woman gave her a hug and whispered, "The place was robbed last night. Bernice must have caught the thieves. They pushed her or she fell, hit her head, and—well, honey: she's dead."

Lateesha didn't remember walking home. For a long time, she refused to talk to her mother or aunt, just sat in her room, staring at the mustard seed. Later her mother came into her room, held her close, and said simply, "I know. I know." Then the tears that hadn't come began to flow.

No one was accused of the crime; it went into the police files marked "unsolved." Lateesha suspected that Tyson was involved—or maybe some of the older boys he hung out with. But she had no proof.

Lateesha, her mother, and her aunt attended the funeral. The church was filled with flowers. Bernice would have loved that, the girl realized.

Lateesha worried about the gardens she and Bernice had cared for so carefully. Several days after the funeral, she went by the house. There were still tatters of yellow police tape, but she went around the side of the house without anyone stopping her. She was half-afraid until she saw the rosebushes and honeysuckle; without Bernice, the green things would wither and die and blow away like dandelion fluff on the wind. She vowed to take care of them.

In the backyard she discovered two women talking. One was the neighbor lady she knew. The other, younger woman, a stranger dressed in a tidy dark suit, eyed her uncertainly. The neighbor put her hands on Lateesha's shoulders, saying, "This is the friend who helped Bernice in the garden." Then, to the girl, she said, "This is Bernice's cousin. Looks like the place is going to belong to her."

"At some point," said the other woman in a tired voice. "My cousin didn't leave a will, so I don't know how soon things will happen."

Lateesha touched her necklace, drawing courage from the mustard seed. "Can I come and take care of the garden?"

"I don't want the property to fall apart any more than it has," said the young woman. "I can't pay much —"

"I don't want pay," insisted Lateesha, "just let me take care of things. I'll do good. Bernice said I had a green thumb."

"All right," said the woman, catching the neighbor's nod. "But the house will be locked. And I'll come by to check regularly."

"Just the garden," said Lateesha happily.

She visited the cottage every day. And the garden flourished. Sometimes, when she was pruning a shrub or pulling up clover, she thought she caught a glimpse of Bernice in her flower-print muumuu and straw hat just out of the corner of her eye. When she turned, there was no one there, of course, but she felt sure her old friend was watching and approving.

The one thing that the woman could no longer do, it seemed, was protect Lateesha. With Bernice gone, the idea that the "witchy woman" could make trouble for anyone who bothered the girl faded. Ty and his friends began to get in Lateesha's face, little by little — as if testing to be sure that Bernice couldn't zap them from beyond the grave. There were spit wads in the classroom, shoves on the playground, crude jokes and laughter aimed at Lateesha on the bus ride home.

One afternoon when she got off the bus and walked the block toward Comstock Court, she was aware that she wasn't the only one to get off at the stop. Looking over her shoulder, she saw Ty and Jerome and another boy following her. She was walking west, so they were between her and home. Not knowing what else to do, she decided to tough it out and go to Bernice's as she had planned. Since they hadn't really done much at school, she thought they might only be trying to frighten her. So she just touched her necklace and kept on walking, though part of her wanted to break into a run. She figured if she didn't look scared, they might give up the game and go.

But they didn't. They strolled along behind her, silently eyeing her, as she pushed through the rickety gate and started up the flagstone path that ran by the side of the empty house. She hoped they wouldn't want to step onto the property where some "witchy" spell might linger.

A moment later, however, she heard the gate creak open

again. When she reached the backyard and began uncoiling the garden hose, she looked up to see the three of them watching from the corner of the house.

"You're trespassing," she said, trying not to sound as scared as she felt. "And Bernice's cousin is going to be coming by anytime."

"I don't see nobody," said Ty.

"Go away, Ty," she said. "I got work to do." But her hands were sweaty on the hose, and her voice sounded shaky.

Ty suddenly lunged forward and grabbed the hose from her. "Payback time!" he shouted, swinging the hose. The nozzle hit her a stinging blow across the cheek. She gave a cry and pressed her fingertips to the wound; they came away pink.

"You ain't got no lyin' ol' witch helpin' you now, *girl-frien'*," the boy sneered. He began slapping the nozzle against his palm, moving toward her as she backed away. The other two boys followed him.

There was no place to escape. They had cut her off from the passageway through the hedge. The only place to run was down the side of the house, where the vegetables grew, and that was a dead end, completely blocked off by a high fence. She rubbed the mustard seed between her thumb and forefinger, as though it could magically summon Bernice to help her.

She stepped backward off the brick path into the massed greenery at the fence that began where the hedge ended. Here a huge hood of passion vine kept all in shadow much of the time, allowing for lots of things to grow in the half-light. There were blackberry vines thriving here; woody, twiny roots of ferns twisting just below the surface; bougainvillea, with thorns protecting its leaves and blossoms; and ivy thick on the ground. Some half-formed thought in the girl's mind made her feel safer in the green shade.

The vines and roots seemed to shift away from her feet; thorny branches and ropy vines drew aside for her. She backed in farther, until the tickle of passion vine leaves on her neck and the backs of her legs and arms let her know that she'd reached the fence. She was trapped. Helplessly she clasped her fist around the plastic bead holding the mustard seed.

Still grinning, Ty and the others moved relentlessly toward her through the shade.

Lateesha blinked, then blinked again. Behind the third boy, she was so certain she saw her friend that she cried out, "Bernice, help me!"

Ty and the others spun around, saw nothing, and kept advancing.

"Ain't nobody gonna help you," said Ty viciously. His eyes looked hard and eager, as those of a snake about to strike. Then he screamed as a twist of bougainvillea snared him around the throat. Blackberry thorns wrapped themselves around his jeans. Ivy knotted itself around his ankles, tripping him so that he fell heavily to the ground. He was screaming for the others to help, but they were in the same predicament—vines holding them prisoner, thorns cutting into their exposed flesh. Lateesha leaned forward, as if to help, and found herself gently but firmly restrained by the branches and tendrils of the curtain of passion vine behind her. Mercifully the green canopy drooped down to the ground between her and the sight of the stricken, ter-rified boys. But through the dense green she could hear their shouts turning to screams. Then one of them—she thought it might be Jerome—began to yell, "It like quick-sand! Ground pullin' me down!" Now there were cries for help from all three boys. The blanket of vines drew more closely around her, pressing up against the sides of her head even as she tried to shake them off, as if they wanted to shut out the cries from the other side of the living green veil. Lateesha managed to yell, "Stop!" just as the sounds of struggle abruptly cut off. She strained to hear, but there was only silence now.

Then, slowly, the overhanging curtain began to raise itself back into the air; the tendrils and vines gradually unwound from her body. When she looked out through the shade into the sun-drenched garden, there was no sign of the boys. The masses of blackberry and ivy looked undisturbed. The bougainvillea swayed slightly in the soft breeze that blew through the garden. Like someone wak-ing from a dream, Lateesha stepped from the shade into the dazzling brightness. She was still holding the mustard seed. Not knowing what else to do, she picked up the gar-den hose, where Ty had dropped it, and turned the handle on the faucet by the porch steps.

Just as the water began to flow, she heard a tapping on the kitchen window overhead. Looking up, she saw

Bernice smiling out at her. The old woman was holding up her thumbs. Lateesha saw her lips moving. Though she couldn't hear anything, she could read the shape of the words. "You got the green thumb," Bernice was saying.

Then the window was just an empty rectangle. Something told Lateesha she wouldn't see the old woman again. That thought made her sad, but she also knew she had a very special gift—a gift that would always link her to Bernice.

Stretching out her thumbs, she could see no difference in them. But as she gazed at her thumbs, there came a deeply satisfying sigh from the growing things all around. It might just have been the breeze, but she doubted it.

Then she began to water the thirsty plants—her friends. Her protectors.

el arroyo
de los fantasmas

There is a dry, brush-filled flood channel in southern California, not far from the Mexican border, that has been the scene of several disappearances—all children. Little more than a narrow passage between rocky walls, with a thin trickle of water from the nearby Mariana Reservoir running down the center, it is a place that superstition clung to, even before the vanishings. Locals shunned the place, calling it *El Arroyo de Los Fantasmas,* or The Phantoms' Arroyo. They claimed that shadowy shapes could be seen moving along the ravine by starlight and moonlight, born in the twilight and departing with the first light of dawn. These phantom shapes came to be known as *Los Veladores Tenebrosos*—The Dark Watchers. The Watchers remained a local ghost story, taken with a grain of salt by the less superstitious folks who lived in the town of Mariana (population 7,000, give or take).

Then things began to happen. In 1958, Jorge Mendoza went for a bike ride with his cousin Alessandro Lopez, who was visiting from Bakersfield. They set out on a Saturday morning, headed for the reservoir by way of the Arroyo. Unbeknownst to Jorge's parents, the boy had spent the night before filling his cousin's head with stories of the ghostly Watchers, then dared him to ride through the "haunted" area.

When the boys failed to return that evening, Jorge's distressed parents notified the sheriff, who promptly issued an all-points bulletin for the missing twosome. For several days, the sheriff's men, police from neighboring communities, and hundreds of volunteers combed the Arroyo and the surrounding foothills. Navy frogmen even plumbed the sixty-foot depths of Mariana Reservoir. But the search only turned up the two bicycles and Jorge's jacket, bearing his initials, in the Arroyo. The jacket—with one sleeve torn off and missing—was discovered some fifty feet from Jorge's battered old Western Flyer Super Bike. No other trace of the cousins was ever found.

After this, stories began to circulate that the Dark Watchers were responsible. The authorities dismissed the idea, focusing instead on the possibility of real-life kidnappers. But no additional evidence was found.

Then, in 1961, ten-year-old Billy Hardesty, out hiking with his family in the Arroyo at day's end, ran on a little ahead of the others, rounded a rocky outcropping, and vanished.

When the family could find no trace, a search began that included helicopters, mounted patrols, bloodhounds, and professional wilderness trackers. But after a week of chopping through chaparral and searching every cave and crevice in the area, the search was called off. The boy's disappearance was never explained.

Five years later, eleven-year-old AnnaBeth Morgan, out on a nature walk with her church group, paused for a moment behind the other children and the group leader as they were returning to their bus at the end of the day. According to one of her friends, who happened to turn around, the girl just stepped off the path, clearly having seen something in the gathering shadows that caught her attention. When she failed to reappear, the other girl grew worried and called to the group leader. But AnnaBeth had vanished into thin air.

Again, a massive search party of police, rangers, and volunteers scoured the region, but investigators found no clues, no suspects, and no traces. It was another case that simply refused to resolve itself.

But these unsettling accounts only intrigued ten-year-old Reuben Castillo and his friends Dolores Perez and Pedrito Gonzalez. They had all been warned to stay away from the Arroyo with its unsavory history. But all the *don'ts* made them more curious than ever to learn what secrets the Arroyo might hold. So, late one afternoon, they set out on their bikes to explore the place. It had been years since the last youngster, AnnaBeth, had disappeared. Yet Reuben, ahead of the other two riders, felt a chill as he entered the

El Arroyo de Los Fantasmas

Arroyo. But he also felt distanced by time from the tragic events of nearly forty years before. When the sandy, rocky ravine floor proved too rugged for them to keep riding, they walked their bikes and discussed details of what had happened in years past, recalling what they had heard about kidnappers, aliens, or Los Veladores Tenebrosos, The Dark Watchers. Such talk—within the Arroyo—began to put Dolores and Pedrito on edge.

Reuben, sensing his friends' growing unease, sneered, "Those are only stories my *abuelo* tells to keep me from coming here." The others looked doubtful, but pushed on. Still, as the hour grew later and the shadows grew longer, the old stories seemed more vivid—even to Reuben. Dolores and Pedrito became more eager to head home. Not ready to call it quits, Reuben mocked them with more assurance than he felt, making fun of the reported haunters, too. He remembered how his abuelo called them *tramposos,* tricksters, who could weave any shapes out of the darkness. But he didn't share this information with his already nervous friends.

In the narrow space between the rocky walls, darkness thickened more rapidly than Reuben had expected. Somehow it had gotten later than they thought. Dolores and Pedrito began to complain about what trouble they were going to get into. Even Reuben, for all his bravado, found himself watching the deepening pools of shadow. Suddenly Dolores grabbed Reuben's arm, hissing in a frightened whisper, "There. Look *there.*"

Reuben stared at where she was pointing—to the west side of the Arroyo, where the setting sun cast the deepest shade.

"I don't see anything," Reuben said with an elaborate shrug.

But the girl would not be reassured. "There are blacker shadows in the dark there," she hissed. "Los Veladores Tenebrosos!"

Both boys now stared but couldn't make out what she claimed to see. Still, her words spooked Reuben (though he still played macho and wouldn't admit to his growing worry).

Suddenly a sound like whispering came from the chaparral and rocks all around them: soft, mocking, frightening whispers. "The wind," Reuben said, not truly believing his own words. But the others were now certain the Dark Watchers had come to claim them. Dolores's and Pedrito's nerves collapsed at the same moment. They tried escaping on their bikes, but sharp stones shredded Dolores's front tire. Pedrito put her on his handlebars. They sped jerkily down the Arroyo, fighting the sand, while Pedrito swiveled sharply this way and that to avoid jagged rocks. Yelling for Reuben to follow, they rounded a turn and disappeared from view. Reuben hesitated just a moment, glancing around; now he was sure he saw a strange rippling in the ever-thickening shadows. He peeled out after his friends, following their zigzag path, grunting as the stony ground under his wheels jounced and jolted him.

He rounded the outcropping moments after his friends—and found the brush-fringed trail ahead empty. There was no trace of the others. He started to shout for them, then stopped in midcry. The shadows on either side of the narrow canyon seemed to be shifting and redefining themselves in unnerving ways—almost human shapes, like the hooded Franciscan monks who sometimes came to speak during Mass on Sundays at Santa Ynez Church. His voice seemed to attract them. But so did the unavoidable *crunch* of his bike tires on sand and gravel.

Something long and dark lashed out at him from a bush. He swerved around it, narrowly avoiding what looked like a thin, black arm tipped with claws rather than fingers. A splash of something red beside the path could have been Dolores's sweater, which she had been wearing tied around her waist. But he wasn't about to stop and investigate. The Arroyo was awash in shadows, and the shadows were alive with whispers.

He bounced over roots and rocks, trying to keep momentum, but it was growing harder as the canyon floor sloped more sharply upward. At last it became impossible to keep pedaling. Reuben abandoned his bike and ran up the path, afraid to look back, sure he would see a horde of dark shapes following him, spindly arms outstretched, claws grasping hungrily.

He was running out of breath, there was a pain in his side, and he could no longer remember how much farther and higher up the trailhead was. He just plunged on, until his gasping for air and his fear merged into the same sobbing.

Then he had to stop for a minute to catch his breath. Far behind, he saw a churning mass of shadows—one and many, like a mob of black-cowled monks pouring up the trail. He scanned the path ahead, and saw, to his dismay, that more of the shapes were clustered where a particularly high part of the ravine wall threw a deadly patch of shadow across the trail, cutting off his retreat.

Desperate, he looked around for someplace to hide, even though he knew it was futile. Where could you hide from shadows? But he took a chance and ducked to his left, where tumbled rocks hinted at a way out of the darkening ravine. He began to scramble up the scree, sending loose rocks rattling down, nearly losing his balance and following them down the scarp. But he managed to keep climbing toward the heights, where the light of the westering sun still tinted the wall golden orange and revealed what looked to be a narrow shelf of rock. He felt that if he could outclimb the shadows, he could escape the shapes that boiled and seethed and clutched at him from within the rising dark.

Up and up he struggled, grasping for the light like a drowning man fighting for air. Another stone gave way underfoot and nearly sent him tumbling after it into the shadows, but he managed to grab hold of a jutting rock just overhead and scrabbled higher toward the little sun-washed shelf that was his goal.

Then, with a final, frantic heave, he threw himself onto the ledge. Panting, he leaned back against the wall, folding his legs in under him, hoping to make himself invisible to anything below. For a long time, he scarcely dared to breathe, watching with growing unease as the darkness edged up over the rim of the ledge and crept across the shelf toward him.

Unable to stand the suspense any longer, he leaned

forward — keeping his head high and in the sun — and peered into the canyon. The floor below was an inky sea of shadow. But stare as he might, he couldn't discover any darker shapes within the murk. Had the Watchers given up the chase? Reuben wondered. Or had he only imagined them? But if they weren't real, what had happened to Dolores and Pedrito? He remembered the red blot of what he was now sure was Dolores's sweater beside the path. No, the Watchers were real. His abuelo's warnings had been correct. These fantasmas were not to be trifled with.

For a moment he was nearly overwhelmed with regret for having led his friends into such danger. But he pushed this grief aside. Now he had to decide what to do next to survive. Even though it seemed that whatever was below him had abandoned the pursuit, he dared not descend before morning, when daylight would drive away any lingering threats. He studied the canyon wall above him, but it offered scant handholds or outcroppings for climbing the remaining fifty feet or so to the rim. He resigned himself to the fact that he would have to spend the night here — unless rescuers came sooner, alerted by one or all parents that three youngsters had disappeared. Then, with a sigh, he realized he had made sure that he and the others had told the grownups they were going to the playground in town, hiding the fact that they were disobeying and exploring the off-limits Arroyo. It might be hours and hours before a large-scale search would lead rescuers here.

Trying not to disturb so much as a pebble, he resumed his sitting position, savoring the last bit of warmth from the sunlight that now reached down only to his waist. Reuben could feel a hint of night's cold in the evening air. He regretted that his Windbreaker was still balled up and clipped to the rack at the back of his abandoned bike. He had heard stories of lost hikers — children mostly — who had died of exposure in this wilderness. The thought gave him a chill that was only partly due to the cooling air around him.

He dared another glance over the ledge. The blackness below seemed merely that: darkness unmixed with unnatural *things.* But even if he was bold enough to risk a descent into the uncertainty, he wasn't foolish enough to try and feel his way down the precipitous, treacherous wall, which was now cloaked in shadow.

Having nothing better to do, he explored his refuge. It was a rough half circle of stone. On the left rose a big boulder. From behind the stone, a fissure extended upward — seemingly to the top of the cliff. It looked climbable. If he could just reach the foot of this chimney, he might be able to scramble to the cliff top and escape the shadow-choked Arroyo altogether. Then he would lead rescuers back to search for Dolores and Pedrito, though he seriously doubted they would find any more trace of them than of the kids who had vanished earlier. Dolores's sweater would become a grim reminder, just like Jorge Mendoza's ripped jacket found all those years before. But no way could Reuben abandon his friends. Flashlights and searchlights would, he felt sure, shield rescuers from threatening shadows.

Looking closer, he found that the boulder had apparently

fallen onto the ledge ages ago, blocking access to the chimney. He tried climbing over it, but the surface was too smooth. Then he discovered about a foot of ledge that ran around the base of the stone. It was risky, but it was his only hope.

Hugging the boulder (more to steady himself than to hang on), he began edging around the massive stone. A shiver of fear ran through him as he balanced on a shelf of rock barely as wide as his foot, clinging to a surface that offered no true purchase. He risked a quick peek down — and wished he hadn't. The retreating sunlight dusted his shoulders. Below, the Arroyo was a stagnant river of darkness. To Reuben's overheated imagination, fed by his very real danger, it now seemed aswarm with shadows — like piranhas beneath the placid surface of a falsely peaceful-looking jungle pool.

He turned his full attention to the immediate problem: making his way around the boulder. The shelf was getting narrower; the backs of his heels jutted into space now. He dreaded that the shelf might disappear before he was all the way around and he shuddered at the thought of retracing his steps without a minute to rest. The backs of his legs, his shoulders, and his arms ached with tension.

Then, mercifully, the ledge widened underfoot. He was home safe. Reuben scrambled eagerly into a wedge of space between the rock and the canyon wall. Here was the base of the chimney. Leaning into it, looking up, Reuben found that the sides were uneven, offering plenty of handholds and footholds; and it tilted back, which would make the climb even easier. To his eye, it was a straight shot to the canyon rim.

"All right!" he said aloud, grateful for a break at last. Then he clapped his hands over his mouth, as if to recapture the words that seemed unnaturally loud in the evening stillness—loud enough to alert the shadows below.

The light was escaping up the chimney; he took a deep breath and followed, ignoring the pains in his back, arms, and legs.

The climb went slowly but smoothly, with only a suddenly crumbling foothold or handhold to give him a momentary start of fear.

He looked up frequently to assure himself that safety was drawing nearer bit by bit. The lip of the chimney—the canyon rim—caught the last of the sun's rays. He was still a third of the way, he guessed, from the top. His muscles were tied in knots; he felt like one big cramp. If he could just find a spot to rest for a few minutes, he could finish the climb twice as fast.

As if in answer to his silent prayer, he discovered a niche in the wall. An entranceway about the size and shape of the pizza oven at the Pizza Palace (the thought made his stomach growl with hunger) opened onto a narrow passage beyond.

He crawled inside and lay facedown on the gritty floor, feeling the muscles in his arms and legs spasm at this unexpected release. In a minute, he promised himself, he'd finish the last segment of his ascent.

But, exhausted, he fell asleep.

He woke suddenly, freezing, disoriented; he tried to sit up and hit his head painfully on the curved, stone roof. The blow slammed him back into reality, and he let off a string of bad words that would have shocked his parents and abuelo.

He began carefully backing out of the tunnel.

Then he heard a sound that was little more than a whisper, seeming to come from far away. *"Reuuubennn!"*

"Dolores?" he answered, his voice not much more than a hoarse whisper itself.

"Yes! Yes!" came a frantic hissing from the darkness he faced. "Pedrito is here, too, but he's hurt."

"Where are you?"

"In the dark. We hid in a cave when we saw . . . things . . . out there. But we got lost. Then I heard you."

"I hit my head," he said to the whispering dark.

"Keep talking. I can follow the sound," she replied. "But it's slow going. I've got to help Pedrito."

"Pedrito—you O.K., man?"

"Yeah, yeah," came a second whisper, not much more than a puff of air.

"Talk," insisted Dolores. "We're at the bottom of something like a rock slide, but it slants up. I think we can climb it. You're somewhere up there. It's so dark, but we can follow the sound of your voice. *Keep talking."*

He inched farther back into the pizza oven. Suddenly his hands slipped over the edge of a drop-off. Stones tumbled down.

"Hey!" cried Dolores, far below. "You trying to kill us?"

"Sorry." He began babbling into the dark, encouraging the climbers beneath. Now he could hear the sounds of them making their way slowly up the slope he could only imagine since everything was pitch-black. "Are there any of those *things* after you?" he asked nervously.

"No," she said.

"You sound pretty close," Reuben said.

"So do you."

"I'm going to stretch my hands down. When you feel them, I'll pull you up."

"Good deal."

He dangled his hands over the drop-off. A moment later, Dolores's hands—freezing cold—grabbed his. She felt unexpectedly heavy.

"I've got you!" he cried. "But you weigh so much!"

"Don't let go! Pedrito is holding on to my belt, but he's pretty weak. We both need help."

Reuben laced his fingers more tightly through hers.

Half pulling, half guiding his friends, Reuben backed out toward the open air. He paid no attention to the way the surface below him scraped his elbows and underarms and wrists. Stones dug into his stomach and ripped his shirt, but he hauled his friends—pretty much dead weight—back toward the entrance. The sun had gone completely, so what little moonlight and starlight filtered into the narrow space didn't reveal much of anything. Dolores was just a blur.

And then he was out in the chill night air. Back on the ledge. He pulled Dolores out of the oven-mouth . . . and began to scream when he saw the shadowy thing, finger-claws twined in his, erupt, like a snail extending from its shell, out of the dark cave mouth into the night.

"Tricky things," his abuelo had called them, "tramposos."

More were crowded on the ledge, waiting. Others flowed down the shadowed chimney. To Reuben, the *hiss-hiss-hiss* they made sounded horribly like laughter.

bookworm

"What is this?" Donald asked. He held out a paperback copy of *Tales of the Incredible* to Albertus "Al" Whitmere, owner of DarkLore Books. On the cover, a spacesuited man confronted an alien that was little more than a swollen, red head on a flat, seven-legged gray body. In the background, a rocket ship, poised on its tail fins, was aimed at an alien sky.

But it wasn't the illustration on the old, yellowing science fiction book that had caught the boy's attention. A perfectly round hole had been drilled into the bottom of the book; when Donald opened it on the counter, he and Al could see that an upended teardrop-shaped space had been carved into the book from the entry hole. A second, perfectly smooth round hole had been bored from the teardrop through the binding of the book and out the back.

Bookworm

The bookstore owner tugged at his graying ponytail as he replied, "Bookworm nest, with front and back door."

"Ugh!" Donald yanked his hand back from the book. Because the binding was so ancient and cracked, it stayed open, displaying the damage.

"Don't worry," the bookman assured him. "It's long gone. Where'd that come from? The collectibles shelf?"

"Yeah."

"I'll have to check the other books for damage. Hope the book came to me that way and I just didn't notice."

"I didn't know there really was such a thing as a book-worm," said the boy, wrinkling his nose in disgust. "People call me a bookworm because I love to read. I thought it was just, you know, a joke."

"Nope." Al sighed. "But I haven't had much of a problem with them. They love really old books. Libraries sometimes have to spray for them in their rare book rooms."

"Worms. Gross."

"Larvae, really. Beetle larvae," Al said. He seemed to be reciting something he had read in a book a long time ago. The man was a walking reference book—like the old character Encyclopedia Brown. Donald had collected all the books in that series when he was younger; he still wouldn't give them up, even though his mother said he'd outgrown them and suggested they be donated to the Friends of the Library sale.

Al tapped his lower teeth with a fingernail—a gesture Donald thought of as the man's way of keying a data file in his brain, like a human computer. "A female beetle lays eggs on the edges of books or on the shelves. The eggs hatch as larvae — people call them worms — and bore into the books, eating the paper, the binding, and gradually changing into beetles. Adult beetles don't bother books once they've found their way out. But by the time they mature, I've got this" — he pointed at the damaged book — "and they're off to find a bride and raise more little bookworms somewhere else. You want it? No charge."

"No way. I don't want those things in my books."

"Believe me, this one's long gone. Oh well." Al dropped the book into a wastebasket with a loud *thunk!* The sound echoed through the empty store. It was late on Friday afternoon; Al would be closing the place soon. Donald had been browsing for an hour, and there had only been one other customer, someone looking for a recently published book that hadn't yet found its way onto DarkLore's secondhand shelves.

"I'm going to get a coffee," said Al. "Keep an eye on things?"

"Sure," said Donald. He often filled in while his friend ran errands — sometimes several an hour — that got the man out in the fresh air and, as he said, "cleared some of the cobwebs gathered from just sitting."

Donald took a stack of collectible paperbacks — books his friend set aside for readers who collected rare, antique, or out-of-print books — to browse (after first checking for worm — well, larvae — borings). He settled himself on a sagging armchair, one of four Al had arranged in a square in the center of the store under a big skylight so readers could catch maximum light—*or minimum light,* thought Donald, since the skylight was never washed except by rain. This far into summer, dust and pigeon droppings crusted the glass, making the late-afternoon light gray. The green-shaded lamp by the cash register on Al's desk and a few scattered, unshaded light bulbs overhead didn't do much to hold back the shadows that, between the tall bookshelves, formed a maze radiating out from the readers' square. There was no way even to see the front door. Al kept all his bargain bin and three-for-a-dollar books there, and even some of these would be ripped off.

A soft, insistent *tick-tick-tick* came from the glass-fronted shelves where Al kept his most valuable books—the ones he sometimes advertised and sold on eBay. Donald suspected that this was how his friend made enough to pay the rent. A few of the books interested Donald—first editions of horror writers like H. P. Lovecraft or fantasy writers like Tolkien. But most of the books were far older, with cracked leather bindings and titles in Latin or German or Arabic. When Donald had asked about these books, Al had shrugged and said, "Books of magick—with a *k,* old style—grimories (sorcerers' books), books of alchemy—occult stuff. The people who buy them call themselves collectors, but I suspect a lot of them are hoping that if they find the right book, they'll unlock the secret of turning lead into gold, raising demons, eternal life—whatever. As far as I'm concerned, the only magic—with or without a *k*—is that people are willing to turn these old books into gold for me."

Donald eyed the neatly arranged books more closely.

It was the only orderly section of the store. And it was the only part of the store with locks, except for the cash register and the doors and windows.

Tick-tick-tick. The sound drew him to the glass-fronted cabinets. He set an illustrated edition of *War of the Worlds* on the stack of books by his right knee.

He still had his ear to one of the glass doors when Al returned.

"Getting messages from the beyond?" he asked, setting down his cup.

Startled, Donald jerked his head back. "I didn't hear you," he explained. "But I thought I heard something inside. Ticking. Like maybe beetles."

"Lord, I hope not," said Al. He cocked his ear toward the case. Then he took out a key ring, selected a key, and unfastened and raised the glass panel for a better listen. After a moment, he lowered and relocked the cover. "Nothing. You're hearing things."

"There's something in there," Donald persisted.

"Well, you never know." *Tickticktick*—this time it was Al's fingernail against his teeth. "Maybe you're allergic to mold in the books," the man said with a grin. "Stuff gets into the air and can affect the brain."

"Sheesh!" Donald strained to hear. There it was—*ticktick-tick*—he glanced at Al, but his friend's fingers were still.

"There!" said the boy, pointing to the case.

Al made a big show of going over to the case and putting his ear against it.

"Nothing."

"You've *got* to hear that clicking!"

"Polter-beetles — ghost beetles. Or their larvae. Maybe only you can hear 'em." This reminded him of something else. "In ancient Rome, *larvae* was the name they gave to evil spirits or the wicked dead."

"You're making fun of me."

"Well, there are some strange books in there. I'll check tomorrow to be sure. In Japan, I think" — Donald never knew where Al's thoughts were going to jump next — "rats supposedly got into the magic scrolls in a monastery. They ate the scriptures, so they ate the magic. They got all sorts of powers. They could turn themselves invisible and all sorts of things. They drove off some ghosts — then drove off the priests. Someday I'll have to check it out on the Internet." He shrugged, swallowed the last of his coffee, and said, "I'm going to close early."

Donald didn't hear him. He was imagining book-worms — larvae — chewing through Al's "magick" books, digesting the magic, turning into evil spirits, waiting for an unsuspecting reader to open the volume and suffer the consequences.

"We're closed," Al repeated. This time the boy got the message and left.

That night Donald had nightmares crawling with mil-lions of beetles and their squirming offspring. He awoke in his room, the book on beetles he'd been reading when he fell sleep resting on his chest. *Tickticktick* went something under or inside the book. Looking closer, he saw a hole the size of a golf ball. The hole hadn't been there before. He raised it up and looked at the bedroom light through it. Then he looked down. There was the same size hole in his chest, as if something had bored down through the book and into his sleeping self. But that was impossible. *This is a dream,* some part of his brain assured him. He stared at the opening, leaning forward to gaze into it. Down inside, something moved—a golf ball covered in green fuzz; the head of a worm—or its bulbous tail as it bored in deeper, toward his spine. He began to scream and tried to raise himself, but something was holding him back. He rocked from side to side, then reached up to grab the wooden headboard, but it crumbled, leaving his hands full of saw-dust and tiny black-brown beetles. Beneath him, the floor cracked and groaned. Looking over the side, he saw only seething, ravenous larvae, swarming up the legs of the bed, weakening the floorboards so he'd soon plunge into a living, squirming sea. There was a buckling sound. One corner of the bed sank. A wave of larvae spilled over the foot of the bed.

He screamed himself awake.

"I should have believed you," said Al. He was sitting on the floor in front of the rare books case, volumes stacked around him. "Another one"—he held up a book riddled with holes, as if someone had shot it full of BBs. He had pulled everything off his Magick/Occult shelf.

"They're all like this. I swear I looked at them not more than a week ago. The dratted things never move this fast. This is so strange."

"Polter-beetles," Donald said. "They've eaten the magick out of your books."

Al didn't look amused. "They've sure eaten a lot of the value out."

"Sorry to have made a bad joke. Are they ruined?" Donald tried to sound extra concerned.

"No—but their worth sure has gone down. Listen: I have to deliver some books over in Marin County to one of my primo collectors. Fortunately I set his books aside two weeks ago, so they're O.K. Marianne is coming in any minute; can you keep an eye on things until she gets here? It's not as if I'm overrun with business." For the first time he could remember, Donald thought his friend sounded discouraged—as if the worms in his books had eaten into his spirit in some way.

"Sure, I'll watch," he said. He could cope if a customer strayed in—but this wasn't likely, since the day had suddenly turned cold and foggy, and not many people were out walking. Al had showed him the basics of ringing up a sale on the cash register. In fact, he had promised Donald a job come Christmas. The boy could even ring up a credit card sale, though most of Al's customers rarely spent more than a few dollars—and half the time the price was assembled out of quarters, nickels, dimes, and pennies.

Al took the small carton of select books out to his car—a classic Cadillac he worked on constantly but which still belched smoke and lurched at starts and stops. He called it Christine II, even though Donald often pointed out that the car in Stephen King's novel was a red-and-white 1958 Plymouth Fury. Donald had been a horror story fan since someone had read him "Tailypo" as a child. How he had shivered and thrilled to the story of the strange creature that came out of the haunted forest to reclaim its tail— which an ultimately very unhappy hunter had hacked off and eaten.

Shortly after Christine II lurched past the corner stop sign and around the corner, the phone rang.

"DarkLore Books," Donald said.

"Who's this?" a woman's voice asked.

"Um . . . Donald."

"Oh, Donnie. It's Marianne. Where's Al?"

"Taking some books over to Marin."

"Shoot! Listen, can you keep an eye on things till he gets back? I got a call from Ashley's school; she's got a fever or something. I have to pick her up. I may have to take her to the doctor."

"No problemo," he answered. "There's no one in the place. I'll probably read till he gets back."

"You and Al—what a pair of bookworms! Thanks, Donnie!"

Donald looked at the "holey" books on the floor. He was tempted to put them back, but maybe Al would have to do something, like spray, or whatever you did for book-worms—larvae. He looked distastefully at the volumes, their leather covers and spines showing the entrances and exits of the creatures. Worms and beetles. He remembered his nightmare. Then he recalled a horror story he had read some months before—one of the few that had really grossed him out. It was about ghostly caterpillars that got into people and made them sicken and die.

He picked up a Little Emily comic, trying to turn his thoughts elsewhere. He sat down in a reader chair.

The day grew gloomier. The light sifting down through the grimy skylight dimmed and thickened, like water in a stagnant well.

The lack of sleep from the night before was catching up with him. Al must have gotten the heater working again, because the air was warm and clingy. It seemed to wrap around him like a blanket. He leaned his head back on the headrest for just a minute, knowing the jangle of bronze bells on the front door would alert him to any customers.

"**H**ey, bud—Donald—you all right?" Al was shaking him awake.

"Wha—where?" The boy was totally confused. Only a minute before, he had been resting in one of the reader chairs. Now he was—where was he?—sprawled behind the counter on a scattering of Al's prized, if worm-damaged, books.

"I think I'd better hire a different security guard," said Al. He was trying to make a joke, but Donald could see that he really wasn't amused. The boy scrambled to his feet.

"Hey, easy on the books—bookworms and now your beddy-bye. These are gonna wind up in the bargain bin if they get any more rough treatment."

"Geez—I'm sorry," said Donald. "I must have gone to sleep, but I was sitting over there." He pointed to the chair.

Al shrugged. "So you sleepwalked. Go home. Get some real sleep. What happened to Marianne? I phoned her house but got a recording."

210

Donald told him about Ashley.

"Hope it's nothing serious. Anyhow — go home." Donald started for the door as Al picked up one of the rare books and peered at it. "What the — "

Curious, Donald turned.

"This is crazy. Look — no holes." Book after book was free of damage. "Maybe we both hallucinated it."

"Weird."

"Maybe I better get these tested for fungi. I've heard of getting high on good books, but this is ridiculous."

Suddenly Donald just wanted to be home. He wanted to shower. He was feeling sweaty and gritty, like all the dust and grime of the bookstore had worked itself into his clothes and under his skin. The smell of old books, which he had found appealing, now clogged his nostrils, clawed at the back of his throat, made him a little nauseated. He wondered if he was coming down with a bug of some kind. The "bug" concept bothered him even more.

Later, in the shower, he kept thinking about the vanishing wormholes. So strange. He remembered something about the idea of wormholes as the water sluiced over him. They were holes in space or something. Some sci-fi writers said they might be tunnels between the stars big enough for starships to travel through. *Or small enough for ghostly larvae to crawl through?* The thought creeped him out. But his mind wouldn't stop wrestling with the idea. What if there were links between the real world and the supernatural world? What if there were a way for power — "magick" as Al called it — to flow into this world? Such energy might use something like wormholes to move through space and time. Maybe things—people, even—could travel through them.

Now Donald was thinking of two old movies—one where a starship flew through a black hole and found heaven inside. In the other movie, however, a ship returned from exploring a wormhole and brought back a demon because the hole had plunged into hell, which was like another dimension.

His mind was spinning faster and faster. What if the old books of "magick" were really just ways of opening wormholes into another dimension so they could pull unnatural energies into this world? And what if—sometimes—something else moved along the wormholes, following the energy into this world? Something like . . . larvae, souls of the dead. Maybe evil dead.

His imagination started whirling in even stranger directions now. Then his father yelled at him to stop wasting water.

Donald turned off the spray, toweled dry, and put on his gray shorts and gym shirt. But troubling thoughts persisted.

"You spend too much time in that bookstore," his mom was always saying.

Maybe she's right. Holes/no holes. Larvae. Evil dead. Demons and wormholes. These ideas ran through his mind as he sat on his bed, reached for a book, and then grabbed his GameBoy instead.

His wrist itched. His shoulder itched. His ankle itched. He scratched.

Bookworm

It felt like when he had visited his grandmother in Louisiana two years before. Donald had made himself a wig of Spanish moss pulled from an old oak. He didn't know — but he sure found out — that the stuff held chiggers: tiny, six-legged mite larvae. His cousin Roger had later showed him some of the things under a magnifying glass. They caused terrible itching. He had to wash with foul-smelling soaps and shampoos to get rid of them. And for a long time he imagined them crawling on him. Chiggers didn't burrow into the skin, but these waking-dream things sure did.

Something moved under the skin of his forearm.

More things moved — like veins rearranging themselves.

Two crossed. A tiny hole like a BB appeared. It didn't bleed — just like in his dream.

Tickticktick (inside his head, behind his eyes).

More holes, the size of black freckles. *None of this can be happening. I've fallen asleep,* he told himself. *I'm having a dream where everything is all jumbled together: books, book-worms, wormholes, worms, chiggers, larvae, ghosts, black holes. I don't feel any pain, so it has to be a dream. But I feel so horribly itchy — could there have been some kind of chiggers in the old books I slept on?*

More holes appeared in his skin. More. When he looked closer, he could see nothing — just black roundness. But he could feel the indents under his fingertips.

This can only be another dream, he insisted.

More holes opened side by side. Some ran together, making a hole the size of a quarter.

Dreaming — don't feel anything —

Something white and fuzzy moved deep down in the largest cavity. He pushed his finger in; it seemed to go straight down—but that was impossible. The tip should have come out the other side of his arm. But it just kept going deeper—like a black hole that goes on forever or at least to the other side of the universe. *Where do wormholes come from? What's at the other end? If "magick" can call beings from that other place, do they have a way of calling us?* That chilling idea had just formed when the edges of him folded into the widening hole, and he was swallowed into a tunnel that was soft and round and long and lightless and seemingly endless.

Suddenly he was rushing down the tunnel, hurtling blindly to where (he guessed) he was being summoned by unimaginable beings for unguessable reasons. *Bookworms,* he thought. *Who'd have imagined this?* Then he was speeding so fast, even his thoughts couldn't keep up with him.

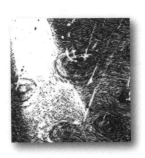

rain

"Tears are your eyes leaking," said Brenda. "I like that."

"Great," said LeeAnne, not caring, hardly hearing, staring out the window at day three of unending rain-rain-rain. The downpour was so heavy that she couldn't see across the backyard as far as the sharply sloping hillside against which all the houses on her side of the block nestled. Watching the rivulets of mud cascading down the slope, she was reminded of TV accounts of towns in California where whole hillsides slid down and buried everything in mud. She was glad that the hills in Michigan were far more stable.

Brenda, ignoring her friend's lack of interest, said, "I read that line in a book. Every time the girl in the story — Maddy — cried, the writer wrote, 'Her eyes leaked.' I think it's a nice way of putting it."

"Put it to rest," said LeeAnne.

"I could loan you the book," said Brenda, undaunted. "It's a good story."

"Like I want to read about some wimp with weepy eyes!" LeeAnne sighed. "We're in the middle of spring break, and we're *trapped here.* Willow Creek has *got* to be the most unexciting place *in the world!*"

"We could go to my house," Brenda offered.

"Big deal—five houses down! My dad's in St. Louis; my mom has to spend all day counseling creeps. And your mom—"

"Doesn't drive," Brenda apologized.

"Trapped." LeeAnne flopped dramatically back onto her bed, then sat up suddenly. "How much money do you have?"

"Maybe ten dollars."

"I've got about seven. We could call a taxi and go downtown."

Brenda, who was good at math, did the addition. "Yeah, but by the time we got there and paid the taxi, we'd only have a few dollars left. We can't do much downtown on a few dollars."

"Call Mary Beth."

"Mary Beast?" said Brenda. "No one wants her hanging around."

"Mary *Beth,* to use her proper name," said LeeAnne, her high-pitched, mock-prim tones making her sound like their homeroom teacher, Ms. Gore, "is a young lady of great potential—"

" —and dress size," commented Brenda.

" —whom it would do you all a lot of good to make your friend."

"Yeah! Like having a teacher chew out the class is going to make her popular." If Brenda's eyes rolled any further back in her head, LeeAnne decided, she'd look like something out of *Shaun of the Dead.*

"Well, she's got a big brain and a big heart—"

"And big bones."

"And a big bundle of money all the time. I'm calling," insisted LeeAnne. "We can ditch her as soon as we get to the mall."

Brenda's eyes did another *Shaun of the Dead* roll, but she said nothing.

LeeAnne pulled on her raincoat and prodded her unenthusiastic friend to do the same. Then they headed to Mary Beth's house around the corner.

Mary Beth opened the door hesitantly, peering at her classmates as if they were complete—or possibly dangerous—strangers. Though her home looked like the other girls' houses, there were differences. Oriental rugs covered the floors, expensive-looking vases perched on accent tables, and original oil and watercolor paintings brightened the walls. A thick atmosphere of politeness, of wood polish, of quiet—and of money—filled the place. LeeAnne and Brenda spoke in whispers, as if they were entering a library or museum. They couldn't help it, awed by such signs of serious wealth. The silence was broken by a sudden howl of wind driving rain against the windows like a fusil-lade of BBs.

While LeeAnne explained the purpose of their visit, Mary Beth kept pushing her glasses back up her nose, which Brenda thought looked shiny with grease. She kept up a nervous blinking of her eyes, while puffing out her cheeks and releasing the trapped air in a series of anxious pops. She looks like a puffer fish on the Nature Channel, LeeAnne told herself.

"I'm not supposed to go without calling my folks," Mary Beth said. Her parents were lawyers. They had their own firm in a neighboring suburb.

LeeAnne smiled. "We'll be back by five-thirty. My mother will pick us up when I call. You said your folks never get home before seven-thirty. Why bother them?" she asked, adding to herself, *and give them a chance to say no?* She gave Brenda a poke in the ribs.

Brenda nodded and said, "Simple; no hassles."

"I guess so," said Mary Beth uncertainly.

"Great!" said LeeAnne. She pulled her cell phone out of her jacket pocket. "I've already programmed in the taxi. You can pay for it. I'll buy us food later." She gave Brenda a wink while Mary Beth rummaged around for rain gear in the hall closet.

The three girls sat in the back of the taxi, LeeAnne and Brenda flanking Mary Beth like guards escorting a prisoner. The willow-bordered creek that gave the subdivision its name was swollen and gray. The cabdriver grumbled at

the rain coming down so heavily that his wipers, revved to the fullest, could hardly swipe the windshield clear of the sheeting water. The taxi *whooshed* through several huge puddles collecting in open runoff gutters that ran across the road or pooled at points where clogged storm drains created small lakes. On either side of the cab, the water fountained up like the fans of spray kicked up by the speedboat when Brenda and her family went water-skiing with Brenda's uncle Norm on the Old Mill River. LeeAnne loved the effect; it gave her more of a sense of adventure.

"I think the driver is going too fast for these wet streets," Mary Beth whispered.

"Chill," LeeAnne said.

"Yeah," said Brenda automatically.

Mary Beth contented herself with kneading her hands in her lap. They were moist with sweat and as shiny as her nose, Brenda thought.

The rain grew worse.

Headlights and taillights were white-red blotches in the storm.

The unrelenting rainfall made the ride into Creek Center much longer. Through the windows, an altered landscape flowed past—familiar landmarks transformed into squiggles and ripples and blurs as their breath steamed the already rain-streaked windows. *It's like being in a minisub, exploring the sea,* thought LeeAnne.

They were on the last stretch of curve around Lake Park when the driver's tires squealed on the slick pavement.

"Make him slow down!" Mary Beth hissed.

"Make yourself shut up," snapped LeeAnne.

In response, Mary Beth suddenly slumped in her seat and gave all her attention to her sweaty palms.

Something bounded across the road. A deer. The driver cursed and slammed on his brakes. The cab spun around twice, like a crazy carnival ride. The girls screamed together.

The taxi came to a stop half off the road. It was nosed into the muddy edge of a picnic ground that ran along the drop-off into Larkey Lake. The driver was making strangulated noises.

"I'm O.K.," LeeAnne said, more to reassure herself than to report.

"Me . . . me . . . too." Brenda sounded equally astonished at still being alive.

"My belt is stuck," said Mary Beth, trying to free the catch. Then she gave a sob that turned into a moan.

"Don't be such a wuss," LeeAnne snarled. Then she turned to look at Mary Beth and saw that the girl, still twisted up in her seat belt, was staring in terror out the rear window. An instant later, LeeAnne saw the headlights of the speeding car behind them just before she heard the squeal of brakes. Then she felt the second car slam into the back of the cab.

LeeAnne had a mental snapshot of Brenda's mouth wide in an expression of disbelief; Mary Beth's mouth was open in a full-throated scream. It was odd, LeeAnne thought, how calm she was herself, her mind clear in the midst of crisis. She realized that their driver had not yet put on the emergency brake; he was only keeping his foot on the brake pedal. So when the impact came, his foot slipped free, and the car shot forward, partly under the force of the collision, partly under its own power. It hurtled across the narrow picnic area, grazing a table and tilting it sideways, before flying off the end of the retaining wall and plunging nose down into the rain-pocked lake.

Suddenly LeeAnne was jerked out of her unnatural calm into total panic.

Muddy, weedy water swirled against the windows and jetted in through seams and holes. When his door wouldn't budge, the driver frantically pulled a hammer from under his seat and smashed his window. Water flooded in. He swam a few feet to the surface, took a deep breath, then swam down and yanked open the door beside Brenda, who was a blur of desperately grasping arms and swirling hair. The driver pushed her clutching hands aside, released her seat belt, and dragged her out and up.

LeeAnne was somehow aware of all this; still she managed to keep focused enough to release her own seat belt, pop the other passenger door, and flail—not really swim—her way to the surface of the silty, scummy, freezing water. Several rescuers from passing cars hauled her up. In their enthusiasm, they banged her side and scraped her knees against the cement retaining wall, but she was free of the muddy waters—dazed, soaked, and numb with cold—but safe.

"Everyone O.K.?" someone shouted in her ear.

She saw Brenda huddled under a blanket; the cabdriver was struggling to dive back into the water, shouting, "There's another kid trapped!" Onlookers held him back while two other men, fully clothed, dove down into the three-quarters submerged cab. A moment later, they brought Mary Beth up. She floated limply on the green-brown surface, supported by her two would-be rescuers. Then other helping hands raised her to the rain-soaked lawn. Somebody frantically began applying artificial respiration.

LeeAnne watched it all as if it were some movie. Dimly, as if on a soundtrack, she heard contradictory advice being given to the man trying to revive the unconscious girl, heard Brenda sobbing, heard the driver explaining over and over why the accident wasn't his fault, heard distant police and ambulance sirens drawing closer.

A woman was wrapping a coat around LeeAnne's shoulders. "I'm sure your friend will be all right, honey," she said.

"Mary Beth," said LeeAnne, shivering, "her name is Mary Beth." Seeing the man kneeling beside the girl's body and shaking his head, LeeAnne knew nothing was going to be all right. Then a crazy thought popped into her head: *We really ditched Mary Beth this time!* The thought was so unexpected, she began to laugh—or thought she was laughing, until she realized she was really crying.

M ary Beth's funeral was held a week later, on a storm-soaked Thursday. Relentless rain dulled the stained-glass windows of the First Congregational Church. In spite of lights and candles and masses of flowers and an overflow-ing crowd (including most of the sixth graders from Willow Creek Middle School), the church seemed cold and cheer-less to LeeAnne. She could barely look at the coffin placed near the altar; she had an awful vision of Mary Beth inside, slapping her palms against the lid, insisting that she didn't want to be dead. LeeAnne buried her face in her hands and felt her mother's comforting pat on her shoulder, but she couldn't free herself of the disturbing mental image.

Mary Beth was buried in a muddle of rain, mud, tears, and a damp cold that seeped into the bones of young and old alike. Under the wind-flapped cemetery awning, with the rain drumming relentlessly on the canvas, LeeAnne and Brenda, with their families, sat far apart from each other. They hadn't planned this. Shortly after the accident, LeeAnne had assured the police officers who gently ques-tioned her that Mary Beth had proposed the fatal outing. It was a small lie, she assured herself, but a necessary one. She had pressured an unhappy Brenda to play along by warning, "Mary Beth's mom and dad are lawyers. They're already suing the cab company, the guy who hit the cab, and the Willow Creek Parks and Recreation Department. Do you want them to sue your family, too?"

"No," the other girl answered dully.

"Then get with the program," LeeAnne insisted.

And Brenda did, though she made it clear this wasn't a willing choice. That was why she sat as far away as possible from her former best friend. In the watery gloom, LeeAnne imagined herself undersea as the minister droned the final funeral prayers, which she could hardly hear over the howl of wind, the loud flapping of canvas like the beating wings of a giant bird, and the increasing *rat-a-tat* of rain overhead. Looking at the half-flooded lawn, dotted with tombstones, she felt as if they were drowning Mary Beth a second time.

It wasn't until three days after the funeral that LeeAnne was able to get Brenda to agree to come to her house "for a talk." Two days before, there had been brief sunshine, but the rain had returned with a vengeance. Waiting on the front porch, LeeAnne felt the insistent pressure of water all around; she imagined it to be like the weight divers must feel deep in the ocean. She was aware of the gurgle of muddy water in sluices, rain gushing down drainpipes, polluted gray-brown water burbling up through the grate at the corner from the clogged storm drain.

The day was uncomfortably like the one when everything had gone down, the girl reflected. At that moment, she saw Brenda splashing up the sidewalk and waved to her. The other girl didn't wave back; she just gave LeeAnne a nod, then followed her inside.

Brenda looked on the verge of crying as she perched on the end of LeeAnne's bed. In fact, she wiped a tear or two away, saying, "I can't help it. I think of Mary Beth caught in her seat belt, drowning all alone, praying for someone to come help her, and no one did. Not in time."

LeeAnne refused to tell Brenda about the nights—every

night since the funeral—that she had fallen asleep to the patter of rain only to have the same nightmare over and over. In the dream, she and Brenda were standing on the retaining wall at the edge of Larkey Lake picnic ground. Rain fell without stopping. Beside them, tire ruts were gouged across the sodden lawn and ended in parallel mud smears across the wall—clearly a car had crossed the lawn and the lake wall and had plunged into the swirling brown water below them. Then the mud-caked figure of Mary Beth fountained up out of the restless lake. For a moment, she hung in the air, balanced on a pillar of muddy water. Then she stepped onto the wall as LeeAnne and Brenda, in the dream, instinctively stepped back.

Mary Beth held out her hands to the other girls. Her upturned palms held gobbets of mud. LeeAnne tried to take another step back but found herself frozen in place. Glancing sideways, she saw that Brenda was locked in the same position.

With a sudden movement, Mary Beth was in front of them.

"You ditched me," she said.

LeeAnne opened her mouth to protest, but the dead girl lunged forward, stuffing her mouth full of mud with her right hand, while her left shoved the second burden of mud into Brenda's mouth.

"No arguments," said Mary Beth. "You ditched me, left me in the dark forever. Now see what it's like."

The hands moved, clogging LeeAnne's and Brenda's eyes with mud, blinding them. LeeAnne tried to scream, but her mouth was filled with ooze and weeds and slime. She was suffocating.

She forced herself awake. The taste of mud lingered.

She shook off the memory, saying, "They tried to save her. Everyone tried." She was aware how insincere her words sounded.

"Not me," said Brenda, more tears leaking—there was no other way to describe it, thought LeeAnne—from the corners of her eyes. "Not you."

"We were in shock," LeeAnne argued. "That happens in an accident."

"It was all because of us," said the other girl miserably.

LeeAnne, sitting on the window seat, her back to the relentless curtains of gray rain, sighed and said, "Get over it. It was an accident. Bad things happen to people all the time. But you are becoming *so boring,* I can't handle it. I thought I wanted to see you, but now I want you to go away."

Standing up, Brenda said angrily, "Yeah, well, I'm outta here. You're a bummer, too." She reached for her raincoat, which was dripping on the carpet.

LeeAnne started to say something more but stopped and looked out the window at the hillside behind the house. A network of muddy streams was flowing down, churning and drinking up the soil, melting it, crisscrossing the slope in chocolate-colored rivulets that in some places looked big enough to be called creeks.

Suddenly, a slab of muddy hillside broke away and slid down. It slammed against the long redwood planter box that separated the yard's upper deck from the undeveloped hillside above. Liquid mud spilled over onto the redwood planking of the deck. "My dad is going to be so mad when he sees that," said LeeAnne. Then, with a startled cry, she said, "What's that?"

"What's what?" said Brenda, in a voice that implied, *who cares?* —something she had picked up from LeeAnne. She continued shrugging into her raincoat.

"That, that, *that!*" yelled LeeAnne, jabbing her finger against the window with such intensity that the other girl was forced to look. As soon as she did, she could see it, too—a rain-drenched, mud-clotted figure, half swimming, half clawing its way down the fast-liquefying slope, which was almost a waterfall now.

Splat! A vast wave of mud slapped against the window, coating it with slushy brown ooze.

The girls jumped back. Instinctively, they wrapped their arms around each other.

From outside, a hand began swiping at the sludge, thinning the mess to brown smears that the rain was beginning to dissolve.

Mary Beth's face appeared, grinning at them with cruel humor. Mud streaked her face and glasses. Though the smile never wavered, tears began to gush from her eyes. But they were streams of filthy mud, torrents of watery mud, rivers of mud flowing down her cheeks.

"Do you see?" asked LeeAnne, aware how foolish the question was.

Too terrified to speak, Brenda could only nod.

"Go away!" LeeAnne screamed at the drowned girl.

But what had been Mary Beth only smiled more broadly through her streaming tears. She shook her head wildly; brown droplets from her face and hair pattered against the window.

"Come on!" ordered LeeAnne, grabbing Brenda's hand, intending to flee the waking nightmare at her window.

Hand in hand the girls pounded down the hallway, then tore down the steps two at a time, each helping steady the other.

They reached the front door.

LeeAnne yanked it open.

Then the saturated hillside behind the house collapsed. A tidal wave of watery mud slammed into the house, burying half the block in an ocean of brown. The last thing LeeAnne saw and heard before her mouth and eyes and ears were stopped with mud was Mary Beth—hands gripping either side of the doorframe, blocking escape, saying, "No more ditching."